AFFINITY HOUSE

RUTH HAY

AFFINITY HOUSE

BY RUTH HAY

Phase four of the *Home Sweet Home* series, following **Harmony House**, **Fantasy House** and **Remedy House**.

Blood makes you related; loyalty makes you family.

The co-housing experiment has been through unexpected changes before, but what happens next, may bring it all crashing down around Hilary and Mavis.

CHAPTER 1

M avis Montgomery decided it was time to do inventory.

She often did a journal noting the successes and failures of the growing year in the gardens at Harmony House, but her present preoccupation was of a more personal nature. She was determined to take some time from the busy life of the co-housing partners around her, and concentrate exclusively on her own health and welfare.

Following the practice of her lifelong friend Hilary, she opened up a notebook, lifted up her new gel pen and began.

<u>Mavis Montgomery</u>

General:

I am coping well with all the changes despite a few big surprises lately.

It is lovely to have my tower room as a refuge from all the drama, particularly when the garden is not available to me. With my books and my music I can create peaceful moments here no matter what is going on around me.

Concerns:

Have I taken on too much?

With Louise Ridley's plans for foster children moving ahead, I know she will call on me for help and advice. Faith is the one best equipped to help Louise but the girl is already over committed at school and with her newly-acquired family members in Kingston.

Thankfully, Eve has progressed very well after her illness and is an independent artist with a supportive group of friends and colleagues nearby.

Hilary, too, is active and involved these days and much happier for it.

Do I have to keep an eye on Vilma? That is something I never thought to write.

Vilma has always been the one who helps others but with her new circumstances

she is in a difficult situation as regards Andy.

Honor seems happier and closer to her niece. She works very hard to make up for

Faith's lack of investment in the house. Honor has not yet asked for my help but it may happen.

Jannice is the biggest surprise of all. She has emerged from her shell in a big way. Vilma gets the credit for giving her protégé much-needed confidence.

Mavis stopped to read over what she had written so far and exclaimed aloud to Marble who was sitting on the table top by the window avidly watching the pen move along and waiting for her chance to reach out a paw to stop it.

"Goodness me! I sound like the chicken that ran around the farmyard saying the sky was falling.

I must learn to concentrate on my own welfare rather than that of everyone else."

She tried to refocus and came up with a new heading.

Health.

This was quite definitely personal. She recently read an article in a women's magazine listing the five life skills for health, wealth and happiness. The UK authors of an eleven-year study recommended these qualities, which Mavis had carefully copied down.

- Emotional stability
- Determination
- Control
- Optimism

- Conscientiousness

"Well now, I do want to ensure health, wealth and happiness. Do I possess these qualities at all?"

Marble did not seem eager to answer. Now that the pen had ceased its fascinating movements, she jumped down and went off to the bottom level of the tall shelving unit where she had a soft nest, curling up until her mistress decided to do something more interesting.

Mavis was checking off the five items.

- Emotional stability........... "One of my better qualities."
- Determination........... "Once I set my mind to something worthwhile I pursue it relentlessly. Of course, this could also be seen as a problem at times."
- Control........... "Now that can also be seen two ways. I prefer to encourage others to gain control rather than impose it upon them."
- Optimism........... "Absolutely my best personal attribute!"
- Conscientiousness........... "What on earth does that really mean?"

She decided to consult a dictionary before trying to determine if she had the last elusive quality and promptly moved on from mental health to a survey of her physical health.

This was of more immediate concern. Although she still moved around with her customary speed and energy, it was becoming evident to Mavis that she was not getting any younger and it was beginning to have an effect.

She looked first at her hands. There was a perceptible thickening of the knuckles on her right hand; the hand that did most of the gardening work; in particular the pulling up of persistent weeds.

This past summer's campaign against the incursion of clover in the lawn had required her to spend hours on her knees and sometimes sitting down flat in the midst of patches of the green and invasive weed. She learned a lot about its sneaky growing habits and could eventually track down the individual plants that revealed a long tough root system linking several clovers together. On a good day, she could extract a foot's worth of weeds at once in this way and it was very satisfying.

Admittedly, it had become something of a compulsion. She was glad when the cooler weather had stopped the need to weed.

Her hand remembered, however. The thumb

knuckle was the worst and it would throb occasionally, warning her of trouble ahead. She had already noticed she lacked power in her hands for tasks like opening jars. Sometimes she moved to place an object down or grasp something and she misjudged the required amount of force. This meant she had to bend down to retrieve items more often than she wished to.

And, of course, there was the recurring intermittent knee pain. That one was possibly more urgent. Mavis Montgomery had observed the kind of devastation caused by foot, knee or hip problems. Friends and acquaintances, including social workers she had known well, were all becoming incapacitated by such constraints. She was determined not to fall into that category if she could avoid it.

Walking with difficulty was becoming a crucial harbinger of approaching old age. Why did no one warn of this earlier in life?

Then there was the matter of eyeglasses. She had always had a pair for reading but now she also had a pair for the computer and a pair with sun protection for outdoor activity.

This was all very well until the business of finding the right pair at the right time became a problem.

It was necessary to have glasses on her face in order to track down the required pair and it was no use placing the various pairs together in one convenient drawer. The latest ones needed to be by the computer, the single focus ones had to be by her bed, and the outdoor ones must be near her purse and coat in case she went out without their protection.

It was not about forgetting where she laid them. Her memory was good. It was just the inconvenience of keeping them where they should be. She often thought it was just as well she did not now live in a house in which she slept on one level, worked in a different room, and watched television in another.

As long as she had access to one functioning pair of glasses she could now quickly find the others rather than having to tramp up and down stairs complaining as she went.

Were these small worries a forerunner of serious illness? She did a quick assessment and judged it was merely a warning. But warnings needed to be heeded.

She was realistic about these small signs. She could not continue to garden as enthusiastically as she had done since coming to Harmony House.

Perhaps she could call on Andy for more help? At the moment, he was almost a permanent resident.

Since his old farmhouse was ruined by rising floodwaters, he often chose to spend nights with Vilma.

If the weather was not too frigid he camped out in his barn, which was on higher ground and survived the flooding, but that was, clearly, not the most comfortable of options for him.

Mavis just had to glance out of her tower windows to check if Andy's truck with the snow-blower attachment was parked near the garages, to know if he was in residence. So far, this had not caused any problems with the house's joint owners but it could not continue forever. A man about the house was a trifle awkward. There was no more wandering around in the morning in nightwear in case they met Andy running out to do his day's work. No one would challenge Vilma directly about this. She had contributed so much more than her share to the successful enterprise that was Harmony House.

Hilary had made no complaints to Mavis but at some point there would need to be a serious conversation about the matter.

Mavis sighed and stood up to stretch out her back. All the experts said sitting too long in the day was destructive to good muscle health. She remembered watching Honor doing yoga stretches in her work area in the lower level. At the time, she had made a promise to herself to pursue the matter with Honor. So far, she had neglected to follow through on that promise.

From a standing position she now reached for a fresh page of her notebook and began a new list.

1. Start yoga with Honor.
2. Walk more.
3. Eat less of fattening food.

It was a hopeful beginning; not too much to accomplish. She made up her mind to be grateful for all the things she could still do and not worry over much about the ones that might become a problem in the distant future.

Wasn't optimism one of the qualities she claimed?

She left the page of promises in a prominent position on the table and went off, with a satisfied smile, to see if Honor was available.

Mavis' mother had always said, "Start as you mean to finish, my dear." Lobelia Kennedy was a formidable woman and her daughter remembered her advice and took it to heart whenever possible.

∽

Vilma Smith started the day by kissing Andy

goodbye. He tiptoed downstairs, boots in hand, closely followed by the dogs and Vilma, who were heading out to the forested area behind Harmony House for their morning run. She preferred this early start. She could pretend they were a normal couple living in a normal house rather than surrounded by other females who were not necessarily pleased to have a male in their midst. Thus far, no one had actually accused Vilma of breaking the unwritten laws of the co-housing agreement. It was intended to be a place of mutual support and refuge for six women.

Women. Not younger, active men.

She comforted herself with the knowledge that the support part of their mission had been truly met and surpassed, ever since the beginning. The good hearts of the inhabitants had meant any unexpected event that might happen could be overcome with combined effort. She thought of Eve in particular, then Jannice and of course, Honor.

The arrival of Honor's niece, Faith, was an example of how flexible the women had been. A fourteen-year-old, unknown, and somewhat irrational girl, could definitely have been refused a place, but that option was never considered. Honor was one of the Harmony House group, and as such, her needs were given priority. She had required plenty of support with Faith and she had received it from all quarters. Vilma admitted she was the last to reconcile with the girl's arrival but now she could see what a difference it had made to Honor to have a close family member in her life. It was also rather interesting to have a young person around to spark them up although some of the girl's ideas had been problematic.

There was another reason why Faith made Vilma's predicament with Andy's arrival less worrisome.

The original six women had bought equal shares in Harmony House.

Faith was not able to contribute any money whatsoever and yet she had been accepted without debate.

Honor covered her niece's monthly expenses and had started a fund from her own business earnings to compensate for the loss of a room in the house that was intended for other communal uses.

Faith had proved to be useful with respect to finding savings in the grocery stores. She recently began to help Vilma out with the dogs but she was, basically, supported by the others in the house.

Vilma did not want to place Andy in this category. She could afford to pay his monthly costs and did so.

He kept the occasions when he shared her bed down to a minimum, conscious of the imposition he represented. She could not join him in the barn. It was impossible for her to endure that kind of deprivation despite her feelings for him. Andy never questioned this. It made him more intent on earning enough money to add to the insurance claim he had made, so that he could begin to build a new business on his property. He could use the barn in its present state to set up his dog-training business on a temporary basis once he had the cash for the necessary advertising.

There were a number of issues related to this plan. Everything was time sensitive.

Because of the flooding in the area around the branches of the Thames River, the insurance claims were not being processed quickly.

Andy's recent success at a notable dog show near Cornwall should be acted upon while that success was still relevant.

Their current living arrangements were not promoting the closeness and predictability a new relationship needed and she could not see a way to change the situation. Andy was too proud to accept her money to speed things up. It had taken serious pleading to make him agree that she should contribute a full half of the share of the building costs for the new house.

Vilma thumped her boot-clad feet on the snow to encourage better circulation and followed along as Astrid and Oscar roamed to the border of their territory. Andy had left in his truck twenty minutes previously but the dogs, in their heavy winter coats, were happy to remain outside as long as they were permitted to do so.

She noticed, Astrid, the leader of the pair, was venturing onto the layer of ice that had formed on the stream. Andy had said to let her find out for herself that the ice would not hold her weight but Vilma stood ready to give a helping hand should her dog get into trouble.

Fortunately, Astrid decided getting one paw wet in the icy water was enough for her and she rollicked back to her mistress' feet with Oscar in tow.

It was time to return home for warmth and comfort and food. Vilma was conscious of the lack of such things in Andy's working day of clearing driveway snow for clients. She made sure he had a flask of hot coffee with him and a sandwich of peanut butter and jam to keep up his energy. She knew he would head back to the barn to make sure the property was secured and the long driveway from the road to the barn was kept clear. He had a hotplate there for quick meals but she worried about his health under these less-than-ideal circumstances.

On the way back through the forest she thought about the kind of house she would like to live in with Andy. It was a lovely site above the fast-flowing stream hedged with willows. The battered old farmhouse had now been removed so the view would be enhanced.

She pictured a charming cottage with large windows and a covered porch. Perhaps a deck and a garden fenced in so their dogs could be safe and free to get exercise. She had a tentative plan for the furnishings; all soft colours and padded seating around a fireplace.

One big bedroom and a study.

Wood floors softened by thick rugs everywhere.

A luxurious bathroom with a shower, big enough for two.

And, a separate entrance on the ground floor for muddy dogs and boots, which would serve a double purpose as a laundry area.

She was most pleased with this last, very practical addition. Not something she had ever had to consider in her previous grand accommodations, but evidence she was beginning to make adjustments to the more rugged environment out in the countryside.

She had not yet shared this plan with Andy. It was too soon.

She would save this discussion for leisurely days in the beach house in Jamaica. That economical plan was almost in place now. The week at the end of February was fast approaching. The paying guests' component had been whittled down from a large group of candidates. The costs would be covered. Andy just had to agree to it all.

Vilma Smith swallowed convulsively as she opened the front door of Harmony House and breathed the warm air again. Despite her confidence, she knew it was not a simple matter to get Andy's approval to this complex scheme. She would have to introduce the initial discussion very soon.

CHAPTER 2

Honor Pace especially loved the early winter mornings in her spacious lower level at Harmony House.

She thought of it as her private apartment. The bedroom and bathroom were small and set against the back wall but the view of the garden through the glass folding windows more than made up for that.

Her dingy old apartment downtown could never compete with the stone patio leading to the expanse of Mavis's raised garden beds and sculptured pathways. The floral extravaganza was ever changing with the seasons and Honor never had to lift a hand to maintain it all. It was Mavis's domain.

As for her own domain, that consisted of a generous space for her desk and computers with storage for files and her own little coffee station and small fridge kept out of sight in the washroom. Everything was on wheels so, if she needed, the entire business section could be wheeled to the side leaving a large open space for other activities such as yoga. The area had once been used for Faith's surprise fifteenth birthday party but that event had been almost a disaster and she did not dwell on it.

Her relationship with her niece had progressed by leaps and bounds since those early difficult days. And now, not only did they have a better understanding between them, but also, they had acquired new family members of a sort since Faith Jeffries used the internet to track down the man who had given her a name and saved her mother from public disgrace.

For Honor, every little thing Faith remembered from those early years was like a knife in her aunt's heart. Honor was guilty of taking the easy road away from their controlling parents but her twin sister, Felicity, had been left behind to deal with a pregnancy and its consequences.

It was not the best start to any kind of useful relationship and the first few months had been extremely challenging for both aunt and niece. It was thanks to a smart young boy named Melvin, that

Faith had found the Mason Jeffries who was the only father she had ever known.

Meeting that man and his family last fall in Kingston, was the beginning of a new era in the lives of Honor and Faith. The girl had settled down remarkably now that she had family links like most other people took for granted. The fact that Mason Jeffries was her father in name only, was not as important in the end as the knowledge that he had worried about deserting Felicity and her little girl over the years. This guilt became even more poignant when he had a wife and family of his own.

Their reunion had given Faith a new outlook and hope for a better future. Since then, she worked harder in school and took on more responsibilities at home. Honor was proud of her progress and Faith knew she had someone who would always stand by her. In time, the dire images of her desperate youth would fade. Faith claimed it got easier every time she spoke up in public about the dangers she had experienced as a child of a drugged mother who existed below the poverty line and exposed both of them to a multitude of dangerous situations. Knowing she was warning others of the importance of good life choices was giving Faith self-confidence and a respected kind of visibility in school that she never thought possible.

Honor knew the girl still needed help, especially with her studies. Once again the benefits of living communally with such a group of wonderful women was the answer. Hilary, as a former school principal had set the standards and Honor was able to supply technology to back up her good work. Together they had succeeded time and again. Faith was beginning to develop aspirations for her own future success and that was the best predictor of an excellent life.

Honor sipped her first of the day's coffees and realized she had been dreaming instead of working.

She had clients waiting online and the stock market results to check on. She put down the cup, stretched out her arms way above her head and promised herself an extra yoga session to make up for her slow start. Lately Mavis had shown interest in joining her for yoga. She liked the idea of sharing her expertise with Mavis. Perhaps Eve and Jannice could join in?

She automatically excluded Vilma. With Andy on the scene, Vilma was likely getting sufficient exercise these days and good luck to her.

Jannice O'Connor was running late. She had heard Vilma leaving with the dogs and presumed Andy would also be gone. She had lost sleep in the night after an interesting conversation by phone with Mitchell Delaney. Remembering it, brought a blush to her cheeks and she was glad there was no one around to notice. Praise of the kind the author doled out so generously, was not something she was used to. It was a real pleasure for her to sit in comfort and think back to the days when her Ma and Da were hale and hearty and the stories they knew from their childhoods came fast and easy. That Mitchell found these stories interesting, and admired the natural way in which she told them, was a surprise to her. The stories were woven into her very being and the chance to retell them to an attentive listener was a complete delight.

Every time she thought back to those days in Quebec City, she was amazed all over again at how graciously she had been received. The hotel was luxurious, the meetings with Mitchell were held in the spacious dining room or the glassed sun room. He insisted on escorting her around the old city and it was a wonder to her how much of past history had been lovingly preserved there.

It was history that enthused Mitchell. Although he was charmed by her old Irish tales it was the more recent adventure involving Jannice, the Harris family, and Eldon House in London, that produced the most excitement.

Indeed, it was a fantastic story and since she had provided the photographs of herself decked out in the splendour of the trousseau hidden in the attic of her old East London home, it was a topic of hours of discussion.

Lately, he had been talking on the phone about his publisher's interest in the finished book. He was planning to invite her to join him in Toronto for the book launch. A local documentary company had shown some interest in a film to be made of the locations and Jannice had made enquiries of Kathleen and Patrick O'Connor to see if they were willing to be a part of this plan.

Luckily, on her Christmas visit, she had asked if the wardrobe that had held the precious clothes was still in its place in the attic and received assurances that it was much too heavy to be moved and they were happy to let it stay where it had been for so long.

There was also additional video material made shortly after the discovery of the garments and permission to use that would need to be obtained. None of this phased Mitchell Delaney in any way. He was a man who liked to get things done.

As she walked through the snow and over to the garage where her small car was parked, it was a happy Jannice O'Connor who took stock of her life and realized what a difference there was today from the shy, reserved and uncertain person she was before Harmony House. All these exciting developments, including her work as a Home Care Provider had come into being through the influences of the women among whom she now lived. She spared a special thought for Vilma as she started the car and drove along the snowy streets, toward the city and her first patient. She was the guardian angel who had somehow seen possibilities in her protégé and fostered all this change.

She fervently hoped and prayed that Vilma Smith could know the happiness in her own life that she had brought to one formerly quiet Irish woman.

~

The clients who pre-paid for winter snow removal determined Andy Patterson's daily routine but he was occasionally asked to do extra jobs when the snowfall was extreme. These requests he would fit in, as and when he could, but his main clients got priority.

It was comfortable in the cab of his truck with the heater going and a local radio station giving him weather updates every fifteen minutes. He had a warm glow in his heart that owed nothing to the truck's heating system. Vilma had added so much to his life that it was difficult to remember why he chose to live like a hermit for so long. She was the bright spark in every day and the warm loving arms every night when he was with her.

Staying overnight at Harmony House was not something he took for granted. He was conscious of the fact he did not contribute financially to the co-housing project. He was there in spite of this. He was never challenged by the other women, but he was not happy to be a freeloader.

If only he had the money to build a new home for Vilma. She insisted on contributing half of the costs but he was a long way from accumulating sufficient money to begin the build. There were still months before ground could be broken and he intended to make use of the time to earn as much as he could. That, added to the hoped-for insurance claim, might make it possible to provide a decent home for Vilma but he knew her standards were high and she was not about to accept anything similar to the Spartan accommodations he had tolerated in the old farmhouse.

One night when they were together, she had said he was punishing himself by living like a hermit. At the time he denied it, but from the different perspective she had given him, he could see there was truth in what she claimed.

For now, his priority had to be the dog training business. Vilma had a comfortable place to live at Harmony House. The sooner he could get the proper facility for dogs in place, the sooner he could start to earn the good money he would need for a decent house for the two of them.

Over the Christmas holidays, he had laboured to recover the stones that had formed the foundations of the old farmhouse. They were the only things worth saving and he planned to use them for building drystone walls to the side of the present barn. Vilma gave him the idea of expanding into kennels for dogs while their owners were on vacation and he could see how perfectly that would work. Canadians were travellers as well as dog lovers. It would be a profitable sideline. The resident dogs would need comfortable, separate quarters with light, heat and exercise areas. He would include a small kitchen and, a bedroom above the kennels for himself and, hopefully, for a future employee. If the training facility took off as he expected it should do, more hands would be needed to help him.

He could see all this in his head. In one way he was reproducing his minimal accommodations again, but it was the only way to ensure enough money for an eventual home Vilma would approve. She loved her two dogs. Living close to kennels where other dogs barked incessantly, would not be her idea of suitable living conditions.

He was certain he wanted Vilma as a partner in all this.

He was just as certain that these delays would need to be explained very carefully to the woman who was used to making things happen by opening her bank account and simply spreading her money around.

Andrew Patterson was not a man who accepted that kind of one-sided help, no matter how hard this interim period would be for both of them.

Toward the end of the morning, he was approaching a client's house, high on a hilly area in a Byron subdivision. This visit was not an early priority as the family were in Florida for the winter months and they required occasional driveway clearing so it was less obvious their large home was left empty.

He lowered the shovel and quickly pushed the accumulated snow to the side of the double driveway. He checked that the nearest homes had similar-sized piles of snow and was about to leave for the long drive back to the barn when something unusual caught his eye. There was a blind rattling against a side door and the inside curtain was trapped in the window.

There should not be an open window or door in the home.

Something was wrong.

He jumped down from the cab and walked over to the side entrance, automatically checking the ground for any footprints in the snow as he drew near to the covered porch. There was no sign of prints but there was definitely a broken pane of glass.

His police training kicked in and he proceeded with caution. There was a slim chance the intruder was still inside the house. He had no weapon to hand and immediately his mind went to the days when King was by his side. They worked as a pair and he always trusted his canine partner's instincts on these occasions.

All he could do now, was stand and listen for sounds inside. He knew not to contaminate the possible crime scene by touching the door knob but he also knew it was his responsibility to inform the police.

A wave of emotion swept through him at the thought.

He had kept all his pain about his lost career firmly contained behind a solid barrier. He even drove around a corner if he saw a police vehicle on the streets. He had separated himself from his former life as a way to keep the guilt and regret at bay. If this current incident had happened several months ago, his impulse would be to drive away quickly and forget any responsibility he might have.

But this was now. This was the new start with Vilma. He had trusted her with his grim story. She had seen his leg burns and she had not flinched. It was time.

He went back to the truck and called London Police to report a possible break-in. He felt relief after he gave the address but he was asked a number of additional questions and began to realize he was a witness and he might also be a possible suspect. There was nothing else for it. He had to stay until an officer arrived. If he went on his way now, the matter would not be easily concluded. A visit by uniformed officers to Harmony House was a possibility he did not wish to risk.

The minutes ticked by. He drank from the coffee flask and kept the engine running for warmth. It was a freezing day and the street was empty of cars or dog walkers. He listened to the radio and tried to distract himself.

More snow expected within the hour.

Traffic accidents in the city, and on the 401 outside London, were demanding increased police presence.

He began to wonder if this situation would permit an officer to come out to investigate a standard break-in report. He could be waiting for hours. Perhaps he should call in and say he was heading for home. He could postpone this difficult business and calm himself down. It might be days before the police got around to checking up on him.

He was taking comfort from this reasonable assumption when he heard a car plowing through the snow at the other end of the street.

It was a police vehicle. Too late to flee.

The officer parked right behind his truck, an old trick to prevent escape. Andy stepped down from the cab and went to meet the officer, breathing deeply of the cold air and summoning his strength for the encounter.

The meeting did not go as expected.

The officer took a good look at him as soon as he came out of the car and a smile crept over his face.

"Good God! I thought I recognized your voice Andy Patterson. Where the hell have you been hiding yourself? No one in the Canine Unit knew where you got to after the accident. It was like you disappeared off the face of the earth. Old Jonesy heard about your divorce but even then we couldn't track you down. The gossip was you had left the area completely. You were missed, Andy. It's good to see you! The boys will be so glad we finally ran you to ground."

Andy was struck dumb.

He accepted a hearty handshake from the sergeant he had known only briefly, but he could not summon a reply. He had been sitting here dreading this moment and instead of feeling painful memories suddenly awaken, he was greeted as a long-lost comrade in arms. The relief flooded through him and changed him on the spot as nothing else could have done.

The sergeant did not seem to notice. He chattered on about the necessity for snow-clearing activity until Andy finally found his voice.

"Look, Mike! How did you get assigned to a simple break-in enquiry on a day when all hell is let loose because of the weather?"

"Ah! First of all, I am off shift and heading home. I live in this area, although not on this street. This house belongs to a retired city councillor and the station's been asked to keep an eye on it while he's away. I volunteered to check it out.

I take it you saw no further signs to indicate there's someone inside?

Do me a favour, Andy, and wait here until I check it out. I'll call if I need help."

Andy watched while the officer inserted a gloved hand inside the broken pane and unlocked the door.

He felt a return surge of his police training and thought he should follow, but he knew he was not employed as an officer any more. Nevertheless, he could not resist moving closer to the house in case there was an emergency. He wished with all his heart that King was by his side.

It seemed like an hour before the sergeant returned.

"Yeah! It's a break-in all right. The security panel is smashed to bits and there are other signs of damage. Thieves searching for anything they could sell fast, is my guess. Nothing unusual. Insurance should cover it.

I'll call it in and we'll contact the councillor for how to proceed.

Thanks for waiting. We've got your number now Andy, so don't expect to drift back into whatever hole you have been hiding in. The guys in Canine will want to see you.

Take care. Good to see you again."

The police car reversed out of the driveway and struggled down the street.

Andy climbed back into his truck and sat for a few moments trying to absorb how effectively this one incident was jump-starting new feelings about himself.

He was not abandoned by the colleagues he respected. He had not been forgotten all those months when he suffered in a dark silence.

One thought came to the fore with full force. He was not going back to the freezing barn. He was going back to Harmony House to tell Vilma what happened. He knew she would be pleased for him.

CHAPTER 3

M avis got an excellent reception from Honor.

"Of course you can join in, Mavis. I'm no expert but you can go at your own pace with yoga. Don't measure your progress against mine. In fact, don't even look at me. I'll push the computers aside and we'll start right away with easy stretches.

No, don't you worry. We'll do five or ten minutes at the most.

I am glad of the break from work, believe me. I need to quit now in any case. I want to be at the bus stop when Faith arrives, to walk her back home. That backpack she carries these days is far too heavy for her.

Yes, your old loose pants are fine. We work on

special mats. Just slip off your shoes. I'll cue up the very first program in the Yoga series and we'll do it together from the computer screen."

Mavis thought it was just as well she was being forced to start right away. If Honor had told her to come back later she might not have had the courage. She plopped down untidily on the thin mat beside Honor and studied the screen. She was determined to stop after the promised ten minutes. That way she could not do too much damage to herself.

The voice of the instructor was gentle and reassuring. It was almost possible to ignore the fact that she was slim and gorgeous. On closer inspection, Mavis discovered the woman was not as young as she had first thought. Somehow, that was making it easier to follow her directions.

Three minutes passed and nothing drastic had happened. It was a matter of holding a pose for as long as possible.

Of course, Honor could reach further and bend more, but then Honor was younger and had worked at this for some time now. Mavis was quite pleased with her progress on the mat.

Next, the instructor asked them to stand, stretch again and try the downward dog.

This sounded more complicated but Mavis tried it. She let her body weight help as she bent forward.

Then she realized she was stuck. She was in the right position, but she could not reverse.

Honor was impressed with Mavis's ability to hold the downward dog pose for so long but she thought it wise to stop at this point. She uncurled her own back, vertebra by vertebra as she had been taught, and still Mavis was holding position.

Very impressive!

A tiny voice intruded on the program instructor's. It took a moment for Honor to realize it belonged to Mavis.

She moved over and turned off the computer.

"Mavis? Are you all right?"

"No. I'm stuck here. You will have to help me."

They ended up laughing together like two schoolgirls, and Honor was glad to see no serious damage was done to Mavis.

"I think I'll stick to walking for a while but I will do the stretches and try yoga again when I am more fit."

Honor did not want to lose this new rapport with Mavis. She respected both she and Hilary so very much.

"Look, I'm just about to walk down to the bus stop to fetch Faith from the bus. She often has groceries as well as a very heavy backpack and the snow is feet deep now. Please come with me, Mavis.

I'll meet you on the front porch after you get your winter wear on."

It was a surprising request, but one that suited Mavis's purposes. She had not seen much of Faith since school began after the holidays and she wanted to check in on the girl in a non-intrusive way.

The bus was running late. By the time Faith descended into the snow with her burdens strung around her, Honor and Mavis had the chance for a long chat during which Honor assured her Faith was coping well at school.

"She seems to have settled down. I give credit to the Jeffries' family in Kingston. They have grounded Faith in some mysterious way and the talks she gives to groups of teens brings more confidence every time she does them. I believe she will tend toward social work of some kind or another and I couldn't be more pleased."

Faith was surprised to see the welcoming committee at the bus top. She happily relinquished a bag of groceries to her aunt and gave Mavis a glowing account of her latest speech to an auditorium of high school students at Westminster Secondary.

Mavis could not help noticing the contrast with

the angry young teen she first met. They said it took
a village to raise a child these days but it had taken
the combined talents of the women in Harmony
House to bring this confident and happy young
woman into being in a remarkably short time.

They were trudging along through the snow on
the side of the road when a blaring horn stopped
them in their tracks as Andy pulled up in his truck.

"Hey! You three! Climb up here. You'll never get
home with all that stuff. I'm heading to Harmony
House myself and I'll clear off the crescent on
the way."

As Mavis was helped up into the rear seat of the
driver's cab she made a mental note to tell Hilary
about the adventures of her interesting day. Not
least among the tales would be a definite account of
the way in which Andy Patterson looked and
sounded like a completely different person all of a
sudden.

She knew Hilary would also be curious to know
what was going on with him and Vilma.

~

Hilary had struggled through two visits to her
'oldies' but returned home before the traffic became
impossible. The radio was advising the public to stay

off the roads until the city workers could completely clear the main streets and side streets of accumulated snow.

She could see how the winters were a particular problem for her elderly people. There would be days on end when it was not safe for them to go outside because of the weather. This meant they must have a supply of food and fuel set aside for emergencies. Her latest driving trips had involved grocery visits and assistance with phone calls to plumbers and electricians. It was becoming clear to her that vulnerable older people needed to plan ahead for these emergency situations and not be caught with dripping taps and broken fixtures precisely when these were most needed.

For several of her elderly folks she recommended grocery stores that did deliveries as well as a company of retired workers called 'Handyman' who were friendly and gave senior discounts for their services.

She had co-opted Andy into snow removal and lawn maintenance for her clients but she knew his talents were soon to be diverted in other directions.

Really, she pondered, *there should be a co-ordinated program to help these people who wish to remain in their homes as long as possible. They can't call on relatives to fill in the gaps. So many families are separated by long distances these days and social services are overburdened.*

She had talked to Jannice about her feelings on these matters and found her in complete agreement.

"The men and women I am employed to assist could do with far more in the way of daily support than I am allowed to provide. Sure now, and am I not always saying how I need to clone myself a dozen times to meet the needs? It's a crying shame to see the lonely state of some of them and know their terror at having to leave their home and go into care on a permanent basis. Do you know, Hilary, there are *six hundred* long-term care homes in Ontario alone. You must be aware of how poorly some of them are run. You just have to read the newspapers. Is it any wonder the poor souls are scared out of their wits?

Believe me, that does not help their health issues one little bit."

As she made her slow progress out of town, Hilary was evermore grateful for the benefits of shared housing. At Harmony House there was always someone with a car ready to set out for the dentist or doctor. There were supplies of food to last all of them through any emergency situation, and a person willing to cook nutritional meals. Best of all, there were compatible friends on hand for talk and sharing whenever problems of another kind arose.

She thought of Mavis with great affection, especially her ability to step up and quietly take charge without causing alarm. In cases like Faith's dire homeless state, Eve's depression and Louise's debilitating illness, Mavis had worked out the best way to solve their difficulties before Hilary was even aware of the problem. Throughout their long friendship, Hilary had learned to trust Mavis's instincts in these matters. It was a great comfort to her to know that Mavis Montgomery was more than capable of keeping their home on a stable footing no matter what difficulties might arise.

It was in this frame of mind that Hilary was not surprised to find Mavis waiting for her arrival, with a pot of piping hot tea and an invitation to have a chat in her tower room. She pulled up a footstool to the couch and draped a cozy throw over her knees as Hilary began to thaw out.

"Well, Mavis, I did not want to run the car's heating at full force in case I didn't have enough gas to get home. The roads downtown were clogged with cars in lineups everywhere."

RUTH HAY

"Yes. Andy said the same when he picked up Honor and I at Faith's bus stop on the way home today."

"Wasn't that so good of him! You know, there are times when a man around the house is a definite asset. What bothers me is that when he eventually leaves Harmony House and takes Vilma with him, there will be a huge gap to fill."

"I do know what you mean, my dear. But for now, just cuddle up with your tea and scones while I tell you some news."

Hilary could not imagine anything more comforting. She gave Mavis a genuine smile of appreciation and her full attention.

"Do tell!"

"This news is from Andy, as it happens. You know how it's not a very long drive from Faith's bus stop to here? Well, Andy was in such a happy state that he managed to describe a whole range of topics in that short distance."

"What? Are you talking about Andy Patterson, the tall silent one who rarely offers an opinion never mind actually gossip?"

"Oh, this is not gossip, Hilary. This is the real thing. It turns out Andy was on a call when he discovered a break-in and when the police arrived it was someone he knew from the London station and the Canine Unit police with whom he worked before his accident, are anxious to get in touch with him again.

I tell you, he is over the moon about this. I have never seen him so animated."

Hilary was still trying to process all the information Mavis managed to cram into one long run-on sentence when she took off again.

"That's not all! He was full of his plans for the dog training facility and he means to start building the attached part that leads from the barn as soon as possible."

"Do you think he feels his former co-workers will help him out with all that?"

"He didn't say anything specific on that topic but I feel it's a definite possibility and just what he needs at the moment."

"Well, this *is* news, Mavis. That poor boy deserves some good luck for a change.

But, wait a minute! This is not going to be good news for Vilma."

"How do you mean?"

"Well, if what he said is true, the house building project is being postponed until the business part of the plan is completed. Vilma might not be happy to hear that."

"Oh, now I see what you mean. But, look at it

from our perspective. We get to keep Vilma here for however long it takes to raise the money for the kind of house Vilma would be happy to live in. That could take a while, I am thinking."

They raised their teacups and clinked them together in an informal toast to this welcome news.

Neither woman had been keen on losing Vilma Smith on a permanent basis. They would never admit this to Vilma, but between them they could take great joy in the way things were working out.

It was one of the best things about living so close together.

Secrets could be shared in private.

Vilma heard the sounds of several people arriving together and she went out of her room and looked over the balcony railing to see what was going on.

She spotted Andy at once and heard the excited chatter of three female voices.

Something unusual must have occurred to bring them all together like this. From the sounds of it, however, it was nothing disastrous.

Vilma was surprised to see Andy arriving back. He had planned to spend the night at the barn but she was glad he would be safe and warm in her arms and out of the nasty weather that was not ceasing after a whole day of snowfall.

She knew Andy would look up as soon as his snow gear was removed. When he did so, she was astonished at his expression. Normally, he was quiet and subdued in the house, not wishing to disturb the feminine vibe in any way. At this moment his face was alight in a way she found both exciting and unexpected.

He lost no time in bidding farewell to the women around him and climbed the stairs, two-at-once, so fast that when he swept her up into his arms she could still smell the cold outdoor air that surrounded him. This behaviour was highly unusual especially since it was in clear view of Honor and Mavis and Faith down below.

She hustled him into her room before things got more heated and she did not have to wait long because he began to talk at once in such an animated way that the dogs woke from their slumber and crossed the room to sit attentively in front of him as he sat on the bed with Vilma by his side.

It was some time before she could understand what he was saying but when she grasped his news she was overjoyed.

"I just couldn't wait to tell you, Vilma! I know these guys. They are the best team anyone could ever want. They have done charity work before and I am pretty sure I can count on them for help and advice, not to mention recommendations. Justin always said I was the best dog handler they ever had. They will spread the word for us.

Do you see what this means, Vilma?

This is exactly the good news we needed to get the project underway."

Vilma, who was rapidly adjusting to this new and improved version of Andy Patterson, could only nod her head in support. Words escaped her for some minutes until she realized he was now referring to something different, related to their building ideas.

"Hold on a minute, Andy! Are you saying you want to delay the house building in favour of a structure attached to the barn? I thought our house took priority?"

Andy came down to earth with a crash. He had not intended to let that little bit of information slip out in quite this way. He began to backtrack.

"Well, it's something I've been considering but I didn't have the chance to discuss it with you, sweetheart. It will bring our finances into line faster if the dog boarding is available sooner. It was your idea."

Vilma Smith was not deceived by his quick footwork. This was definitely a change of plan.

In her past life she might have exploded at this disappointing news, but time and experience had taught her a thing or two about handling men and she swallowed her first impulse and quickly grasped the opportunity this presented.

"I see what you mean, Andy." She paused.

"There are one or two things that come to mind, however.

The first is personal. I could not be more pleased about this contact with your work buddies. I can see this is very important to you. It's a real sign of healing the past trauma the accident caused you."

He laid his head on her shoulder as the words sunk in. She was right. This was the beginning of a new start for him and he had Vilma by his side. Perfect! More perfect than he could ever have imagined a few short months ago.

The dogs sensed the drama had passed and moved off to their feeding dishes in the washroom to see if it was time for a snack.

Vilma was not finished yet. She had to take advantage of his vulnerability but in the nicest possible way, of course.

"The other thing is the matter of sharing my room here at Harmony.

No! Nobody has complained. They understand our situation, Andy, but it will be a longer time until we have a house we can share and I don't want you getting sick trying to work and live on a construction site in the winter. We are just at the start of our shared lives and these are not the best of conditions for that, you must admit.

I am not being negative. You need to continue to rest here and be fed properly here with me, but I do have an idea for a lovely break away from winter for both of us."

She swallowed. It was essential to capitalize on his present good humour.

"At the end of February we can go to Jamaica for one week. Think of it as a honeymoon of sorts. It will be a breathing space for the Harmony residents and, trust me, Andy, it won't cost us a thing. I have an idea to cover the costs completely.

Now, please think of it like this; a whole week together in the sunshine to plan our future. When we come back to Canada the worst of winter may be over and we can move ahead with renewed energy.

What do you think, my darling?"

When she looked up at him with that little-girl expression, he was lost, but he knew his practical brain had to take precedence over his emotional responses.

The holiday week was not a new idea. She had made references to it in the past months and, with the pace of events since the dog show in November, it was true that they both needed a break.

He would try to do as much as possible at the barn site, weather permitting. Jamaica was something to work toward; a reward for them for hard work and effort.

In the back of his mind, he knew they had managed very little time together; a couple of nights here and there. It was not enough to base a lifetime on. A week in each other's company, hour by hour, would set the seal on their compatibility or else demonstrate that their differences were so enormous their plan for the future was an illusion.

It was a huge risk to take. Possibly, this risk was better taken now, before gigantic amounts of money were committed for a brand new house.

He recognized this was a mercenary approach. Not something he would ever willingly confess to Vilma.

There were huge discrepancies in their finances. That was the truth. His business had to be the priority or else he would be a lame dog in this relationship, dependent on handouts from her superior finances. That was an impossible situation for him. One he would resist at all costs.

These competing thoughts swirled through his mind.

Each one was relevant.

What was the consensus?

Vilma was waiting for an answer. Her gaze on his face was unwavering and she could see a multitude of thoughts coming and going through those deep green eyes. The Jamaican holiday was not truly essential, when all was considered. He might well think of it as a lingering symptom of her prior life in which such extravagant fripperies were a regular thing.

If he refused, it was not a death knell, far from it, but it was part of her plan to make their lives easier. Unrelieved constant work and worry was not a good foundation for a lasting relationship and that lasting relationship was her aim in all this.

What was his decision?

Endless moments were passing while he held her life in his hands.

His answer was actions, not words.

What she offered was far beyond a holiday in the sun, and he knew it. Vilma Smith was his future. Only a few months before, when he was drowning in the depths of despair, he could never have imagined the kind of future she promised him.

This was no time for hesitation.

He folded her into his arms and gently pushed her back onto the pillows. His lips and his body would assure her of his commitment in ways his words alone could never achieve.

Snow was still falling, enveloping Harmony House in a soft blanket. They were cocooned in its silence and wrapped safely in its comforts.

The house's residents went on about their business while worlds collided in Vilma's suite.

The dogs happily made use of this unsupervised opportunity to tear open a bag of chews and feast on the contents in the knowledge that later there would be a run in the snow to look forward to.

Life was good.

CHAPTER 4

Andy was her hero. He took the dogs out late at night and again in the early hours before he went to work, leaving her to sleep in the tumbled bedclothes in perfect peace and comfort.

She loved Astrid and Oscar but it was glorious to be relieved of their relentless routine once in a while.

She had gladly turned her face up for a kiss when Andy left for the day, then she had gone back to sleep with the dogs at her feet for extra warmth.

An hour later, as she sleepily gazed toward the windows she became aware that the snow had finally ceased falling and a bright sun was beckoning.

She felt rejuvenated in body and mind, and a host

of urgent activities called to her. First, there would be an enormous breakfast to restore her energy.

When she reached the kitchen she was surprised to see Eve loading the dishwasher.

"Hello stranger! Haven't seen much of you lately."

"I've been busy painting outdoor scenes around London for the Art Show and Sale at the Byron Memorial Library. It's been a bit of a challenge painting in the winter but it's made me realize I can do more than pretty flower paintings when I need to. There's no way of knowing if the new ones will sell as well as the others. The group has been so supportive to me. I really enjoy their camaraderie."

"Well done, Eve! I love your work. When Andy and I build our house I will commission a series of paintings from you and I mean to advertise them to dog owners who come for training."

"Oh, I don't think I could do animal portraits, Vilma. That's a specialized skill."

"There's time yet. Why don't you practise on my two, and see what happens? After all, it's about a keen eye for detail and you have that all right."

"Thanks for the suggestion, Vilma. I will give it some thought after the art sale.

By the way, I fed Andy a good breakfast earlier this morning and he insisted on leaving some for you in the warming oven.

Now don't look at me like that! The money you gave me for groceries is nowhere near used up yet.

You should probably know that Mavis is adding more to that fund as a thank you for all Andy does around here.

Don't worry! We all love seeing you two so happy together."

Vilma hid her blushes as she bent to retrieve plates from the oven. She believed she was hiding her feelings well, but living in close contact meant there were few secrets.

As she began eating the crisp bacon with scrambled eggs kept moist in an ovenproof casserole, Eve lifted pancakes out of the toaster and heaped them on her plate.

Vilma turned her private thoughts to one secret she was concealing from everyone, including Andy.

She had promised to fund the Jamaica week without needing any of their cash, and that complex process had been occupying her time for some weeks now.

As soon as she finished eating, she must review her findings for the final time and make a choice.

As Vilma reached her room, Faith arrived to take the dogs out. It was a professional development day at her school and she said she needed practise with dog supervision. This was all part of Vilma's plan to escape for the week in February. So far, nothing untoward had happened when Faith was in charge.

Oscar and Astrid seemed to enjoy her enthusiasm and the girl was progressing well with hand signals and commands. If she proved to be a good substitute handler, it would be another step along the path of persuading Andy to take the holiday, which she now thought of a honeymoon of sorts.

The trio set off for the woods and Vilma immediately opened her computer and re-read her research.

She discovered there were more versions of co-housing than she had realized. Large and small units were springing up here and there in Canada and they were becoming more specialized. She had not yet found a governing body with centralized information. What she wanted to know was if there existed a format where residents could exchange their accommodations on a temporary basis with others in a similar situation somewhere else in the country.

The nearest she had found to this was co-living /co-working spaces for what was termed 'digital nomads'. These modern-day nomads seemed to be young professionals who chose to work and travel in diverse locations all over the world. Some gave up their prior living conditions completely to fund a membership to the particular company they preferred. To her surprise, Vilma found these companies were proliferating to serve the needs of this coterie of young, footloose clients who simply moved in, plugged in their devices and began working and playing with their new friends on a one-month lease.

Vilma sat back to consider the appeal of this new lifestyle.

For people used to networking with others in the technology business, it was a given that the wider their contacts the more they would prosper. It was a Millennial lifestyle, perfectly suited to singles or couples not ready or willing to enter the housing market.

As she searched this subject, eight options popped up on her screen. She read through the basic costs and exotic locations and thought it was something incredible for those who wanted to try it and had the confidence to roam the world alone.

Faith came to mind. She had few ties to keep her in one place. This type of experience would be an international education surpassing anything a university could provide.

It was an interesting sideline; but not what she needed to find for her present situation.

She had sent out enquiries across Canada seeking two people willing to rent a week in a luxury villa in Jamaica with the benefit of having the owner on site and able to provide advice about all the island's best features.

What she hoped to find was a couple who were compatible in the short run, but who might also be willing to take over Vilma's ensuite bedroom at Harmony House.

She was hedging her bets with this scheme. She was aware that the years of experience in two marriages had brought her a certain wisdom. Nothing in the state of marriage was guaranteed. If, God forbid, Andy found fresh pastures with a younger woman, she needed security and Harmony House was, undoubtedly, the most security she had ever known. Vilma Smith was not willing to relinquish that security until she was absolutely certain it was no longer required. In addition, she was not happy leaving a gap in the finances of the residents in Harmony House which might take a long time to fill.

With all these provisos in mind, she began to look at the online responses to her original enquiry.

The most likely candidates fell into two

categories. Couples who were friends and who needed a holiday in a peaceful spot without huge costs involved, and other pairs who were interested in a fun time with amenable company.

The latter group sounded like party people. Did she want to share her accommodation with party people who were there for a 'good time'? She and Andy needed to concentrate on their own issues and not be distracted by keeping an eye on others who might not fit in with the casual vibe of the isolated beach.

She looked again at the friends' replies and decided to ask them for more details on their situation. She was expecting to charge them a reasonable sum of money for the week's rental in the hopes it would cover most of the costs of her own cottage. As for plane fares, she had airline points she could use to defray those costs. If Andy were willing to drive to Toronto, the week would be almost free of expenses other than food, which in a hot climate was not a big deal.

She sent off two similar email enquiries and sat back. She had done everything she could for now.

As Vilma poured hot coffee into a mug, she suddenly

heard her name shouted out. It sounded like "Help! Vilma help!"

Abandoning the drink she went to the upper balcony and looked over to find a frantic Faith standing in the front entrance calling to her.

"It's the dogs. They're gone!"

She did not waste a moment to ask for details. She ran down the stairs and pushed her feet into her boots and was out the door still fastening her winter coat and pulling out the gloves always kept ready in her pockets.

Faith raced away toward the woods and Vilma had to keep up to hear her story.

"Everything was going well. I kept the leashes on as you said. We were well into the woods. They were on the path as usual and we were getting to the stream. I called them to turn around for home and all of a sudden they just disappeared."

"What do you mean, Faith? How could two big dogs just disappear?"

They reached the edge of the woods and pounded along the track where Faith's footprints, and the dogs', were clearly marked in the snow.

"I don't know Vilma! I don't know! One minute they were at the stream and the next they were gone.

I am so sorry!"

"There must be a reason. Show me where you were standing."

Faith led the way to the edge of the stream and they both examined the ground.

"The only explanation is that they crossed over. Look! You can see their prints going up the ridge on the other side."

"But the water's almost completely frozen over. How did they do it?"

"I guess that's how. The ice is thicker. If they were running fast they could skip over before the ice broke. The question is, why?

Did you see or hear anything unusual, Faith?"

"I don't think so. It's so quiet in here. I was looking around for a moment and then they were gone.

I called them right away, but nothing. I am so sorry."

Vilma's heart was pounding. Faith was not to blame for this. She should not have been left alone with the responsibility of the dogs this soon.

"Look, Faith, it's not your fault. The dogs will come home when they are hungry and cold. I will wait here and think about what could have caused them to behave so badly. You are shivering. Go back home and get warmed up. I'll find them, don't worry. Go! Go!"

Faith turned for home with tears in her eyes.

As soon as the woods were quiet again, Vilma began to listen and to think.

No sounds broke the silence to indicate where the dogs might now be.

She pulled up her pant legs and stuffed them into her boots, then waded carefully across the stream to the opposite bank breaking ice as she went. She was looking for clues.

She soon found the reason for the dogs' escape. There were a few imprints of a different kind to their paw prints. They were smaller and deeper. A deer had stood on top of the ridge for a moment.

Astrid and Oscar either saw or smelled it, and the chase was inevitable.

Andy always declared that dogs were pack animals and their hunting instincts were predominant.

The stream was the border of the Harmony House property and Vilma had not ventured beyond it. There were no other houses past the crescent's four, as far as she knew. It was likely more trees and rocks ahead with no track or path to guide her.

She knew enough to go carefully. Breaking a leg or twisting a foot at this point was not going to help find the dogs. She studied the snow for dog prints and soon found them. There were only a few deer prints and those were very far apart indicating the deer was bounding away from the dogs at top speed.

When she reached the highest point on the ridge, she stopped and gathered her breath for the whistle Andy had taught her. It would travel well in the cold air. It was a signal to the dogs to return to base. As long as they were still within hearing range they should respond.

The sound of the whistle was massive. Snow dripped from the branches of the nearest tree as if in protest to this invasion of the accustomed silence.

Vilma stood with ears on alert for seconds on end.

She could hear nothing.

A frozen branch cracked nearby in the cold air and she jumped in alarm.

After what seemed like an age, she tensed. Was that a distant bark?

She summoned the energy to whistle once more and was rewarded with a bark that must be nearer.

Sure enough, a snow covered form emerged from a distant clump of trees and bounded through the snow to where she stood. At once, she knew there was trouble.

Astrid was on her own.

No Oscar in sight.

And Astrid's leash was gone.

The female dog was agitated. She began to move away and then return to Vilma's side. She wanted Vilma to follow.

This was a more dangerous venture and Vilma was unsure if she should go back and get help first. Something about Astrid's manner convinced her there was no time to waste.

She tightened the tie under her chin to secure the hood of her coat. She was conscious of the cold seeping into her damp boots and knew she must turn back for home soon to save herself.

She pulled her fur-lined gloves high up onto her wrists and bent down to hold Astrid's face.

"Find Oscar for me! Find Oscar!"

Astrid was off at a fast rate but she turned to see if Vilma was following along and adjusted her speed accordingly. Soon Vilma lost all sense of direction. She was relying on the dog to get her where she should be and, hopefully, to get her home again. She cursed the lack of a cell phone in her pocket.

She had left Harmony House too fast to think ahead.

They finally crossed down from the ridge toward the stream again and now Vilma could hear a whining sound coming from a thicket of bushes.

Astrid headed straight there and disappeared into the bushes. Vilma came up as soon as she could and saw the problem immediately. Oscar had managed to get himself caught by his trailing leash which was wrapped around the bush showing how hard he had tried to get loose again.

On closer inspection, she saw how the leash had also twined around his neck leaving him helpless.

Astrid must have lost her leash somewhere along the way, which had kept her safe from entanglement.

Astrid lay down in the snow beside her brother and licked his face to comfort him.

Vilma went down on her knees in the limited space that was left. She longed for a sharp knife or pair of scissors but without either, she knew the leash would have to be carefully unwound from Oscar's neck. It was a difficult operation. To complicate matters further, the snow began to fall again.

She removed her thick gloves and quickly found out the bush had long thorns.

There was no time to waste. Making soothing noises she tracked the end of the leash to where it was lying under Oscar and pulled it out slowly. It was vital not to alarm him further. A struggle would tighten the stricture and could cut off his breathing completely.

She studied the tangle that was holding him and slowly followed the pattern toward his neck. As soon as her fingers could safely reach the clip attached to his collar she unfastened it although her fingers were almost too cold to apply the needed pressure.

Immediately he could breathe again and he attempted to stand.

Holding him back with one hand she unwound the rest of the leash and put it into her pocket.

She saw no injuries on Oscar other than some spots of blood on his muzzle where thorns had pierced his tender skin. He was cold from lying immobile for so long but he stood and vigorously shook his fur into place.

Astrid danced around him and Vilma took a moment to reassure them both.

She looked around and about and knew she was lost in these woods. If the dogs could not find their way home, she would soon succumb to the cold.

Their tails were wagging and they were clearly pleased to have found their lost owner. Vilma did not have the heart to chastise them. They were trying in doggy terms to tell her about the chase and all the excitement it caused.

She clipped the leash back onto Oscar's collar and led him toward the stream. Astrid followed along. Vilma was hoping the stream would eventually connect with the woods that she knew, although at some point they would need to cross back to their own side again.

She hoped her strength would last that long. With the first flush of excitement now fading, she felt the beginning of numbness in her hands and feet and knew her brain was not as sharp as it should be.

For a while, fear drove her on.

Astrid took the front position and as long as she was following the stream, Vilma trudged on. Oscar did not pull away as he might have done. He, too, was cold and tired from his ordeal.

The snow continued to fall and obliterated any landmarks she might have recognized.

Her steps faltered more than once and she almost stumbled into the stream when stones beneath her boots caused her to trip.

Oscar saved her then by pulling up strongly on the leash.

It seemed to be getting darker in the woods. She thought it might have been better to walk on the ridge closer to light from the sky but that option was far behind them now.

Lift a foot and place it down again became the only thing she could think about.

Lift and place. Lift and place.

Every now and then she looked up in hopes of seeing something familiar.

How far had she gone with Astrid? How long had she been trudging along the stream. Had she already crossed over?

She realized her brain was slowing down. She had no feeling in her feet and her hands were icy inside the gloves. She needed to stop and rest but she vaguely recalled a story in which a man lay down in the snow and fell asleep and never awakened.

This made her shake her head to bring her brain online again but in only a few minutes she felt worse.

Suddenly, against all hope, the sound of a whistle rang out in the snowy silence.

At once, both dogs' ears perked up and Astrid took off at top speed toward the source.

It must be Andy! No one else could whistle like that.

Relief washed through Vilma and with the last strength that the adrenaline provided she called out to him.

"Andy! Here!"

As the air left her lungs she collapsed onto the snow releasing Oscar who bounded away after his sister.

The next thing she knew she was being hefted up

onto a broad shoulder as Andy crossed the stream in two steps and began running back through the woods jolting her entire body every time his feet touched the path. He was talking to her but she could not seem to focus on the words.

She was safe in his arms again.

CHAPTER 5

A doctor was called for Vilma. He declared she was suffering from exhaustion and exposure but she was healthy and would recover soon without further help other than bed rest and hot drinks for a few hours.

Faith paraded back and forth along the balcony outside Vilma's room until Hilary told her she was wearing a line in the new carpeting and she should go downstairs and do her homework.

She did as she was told, but she kept her room door open and snagged Andy on his way out.

"How is she?

Have the dogs recovered?

Did you tell her how sorry I am?

Does she hate me?

Can I do anything to help?"

Andy stopped the barrage of questions by raising his hand and signalling to Faith to join him in the dining room for a minute.

"The best thing you can do now, Faith, is to leave Vilma in peace to recover. She is grateful to you for calling me on my cell phone and neither of us blames you for what happened. It was an unfortunate set of circumstances. Chances are good, the dogs would have behaved exactly the same way no matter who was in charge of them."

"Oh. Thank you! I do like the dogs a lot. I would hate for anything bad to happen to them."

"The dogs are fine, Faith. They are camped on the bottom of Vilma's bed and fast asleep.

I am going out to attend to some business but Jannice and Mavis are hovering around in case Vilma wakes up and needs food or something. I'll be back later to take the dogs out.

You can relax. You did fine. No harm done.

On second thoughts, I'll knock on your door later. You should come with me when I take the dogs out for their final run of the day. It will be good for the dogs to see us together and understand they must also obey you, Faith."

Andy would have preferred to stay by Vilma's side until she awoke but he had an important meeting at a bar in town with some of the guys from his team. The invitation had arrived immediately after his encounter with Mike in the councillor's driveway. He figured it had to be a conference call since the voices of his old team were constantly interrupting and asking questions.

Finally, Brady told them all to 'can it!' and took over the call.

"Look Andy! There's a lot to catch up on. Meet us at Bernie's on Friday night. The usual corner table.

Whoever's not on duty will be there for sure. Now don't let us down, you hear me?

It's been way too long, buddy."

Andy glanced at his watch. He had just enough time to make it to Bernie's Bar and Lounge. Fortunately it was at the west end of town and not far. His truck would make it and he need not be away from Vilma for too long. He meant to try the waters with the guys and see how things were. He was prepared for some awkward questions but, on the whole he had more good news than bad to relate. He knew it would have been a different story only a few months ago. *That* Andy Patterson would never have dared expose himself in his dire state, to the men who knew him better than he knew himself.

A warm glow was starting inside him that had nothing to do with the heater running at full blast to dry out his boots and clothes. If all went well tonight, the final part of his life would slot into place. Yes, he had apologies to make to these good friends but Vilma was safe. He had a future to look forward to once again. He had friends and a family who cared at Harmony House and a business he knew he could succeed in.

He heard the sound of hearty male laughter ringing out as soon as he parked the truck and he knew this was a day he would never forget.

Two beers in and it was as if he had never left the team. He berated himself silently as he looked around the table at the guys, smiling and relaxed. This camaraderie had always been available to him. It was his feeling of failure that had caused him to reject the kind of help these men represented.

After plates of bar food had been consumed, the mood turned more serious and Andy was ready.

"Look, you lot are too polite to ask but I want to explain my behaviour to you.

Let me start by saying I am now in a good place. I have had help to turn my life around and there is a special lady with me now."

He was interrupted by shouts of approval and congratulatory back slaps.

Brady took a turn to add, "You don't owe us any explanations, Andy. We know you had hard times and we were aware of some of it, but we stayed in the background until you were ready. The only question you really need to answer is; are you going to join the team again?"

This was the difficult part. Andy launched into it at once. If he hesitated for a moment he knew he would not be able to control his emotions.

"I will never forget you guys. I loved my years with you. When King went, something died in me. I can't go back to who I was then. The good news is that I am starting a new business of training dogs for shows and possibly for services to handicapped people. I have a big red barn outside town and I am about to build onto it. My name is in big letters across the barn so no excuses when you look for it. All of you are invited to see it. My truck has a snow plow on front so bad weather access is no problem."

"Yeah! Mike told us you were doing outdoor stuff. This is great news Andy!"

Johnny jumped in after looking around the table and gauging the amount of support he could muster.

"We will do better than that, Andy boy! Put us to work. Reid here, was a builder before he joined the team. Paul can lift anything made of wood and the prize of the night goes to Russell."

Andy could see there had been discussions among the team before he arrived. Russell was ready and willing to make his contribution.

"Andy, my brother-in-law works in promotions. He'll design a campaign for you when you are ready to advertise your services. Minimal costs only, and I'll be happy to circulate posters or whatever you need."

Andy was speechless. These men all had private lives with family and children. They worked erratic hours in dangerous circumstances and yet they were willing to volunteer their help to a former colleague who had ignored them for far too long.

Brady took one look at Andy's face and called for another round before Andy could say a word.

The difficult moment passed. Andy took a deep breath to steady his nerves and said, "This round's on me and thank you guys. You are the best."

When he returned to Harmony House he gave a full report to Vilma after assessing her condition.

She said she had gone to the washroom unaided and although her legs were still wobbly, she felt much better than the last time he saw her.

"Good! I am camping out on the floor here tonight in case you need anything. I am taking Faith out with the dogs for their final turn and after that, there will be no talk or discussion, only sleep.

I'll take the dogs in the morning again before I go to work and when you are feeling up to it, Vilma, we need to have a serious discussion about future plans. Plus, my darling, I have some good news to share."

Vilma nodded her head. This was a revitalized Andy. He had purpose and energy above anything she had previously seen in him.

It was a sign that things would move ahead swiftly now.

She lay back against her pillows and closed her eyes hoping to dream of the house she wanted to create for herself and Andy and their dogs.

Mavis let Vilma sleep until she woke late in the morning. She checked on her every couple of hours after Andy had left with the dogs and later with his truck. Faith had a snow day off school and she took over the feeding and exercise of Astrid and Oscar so Vilma could get all the rest she needed.

When Vilma arrived in the kitchen she found

Faith sitting on the couch, working on her laptop, with the dogs spread out in front of the gas fire.

It was good to see the dogs so comfortable with Faith, particularly after the events of the day before. Everyone seemed to have recovered. Vilma felt good. She ate like a horse and joined the group in front of the fire stretching her toes to the heat.

Hilary soon appeared to see how 'the patient' was doing.

"I am feeling great, Hilary. It looks like this is a day off for everyone except Andy. Could I ask you for a piece of paper and a pen? I have some notes to make and Faith here is inspiring me to get it done."

Hilary was glad to help but Faith turned her laptop slightly so Vilma could not see what she was doing.

She had resolved to make one final contribution to her vlog and she was composing a letter she would read online. It was titled; *Letter To The Father I Never Knew.*

The idea came to her a few days after she was approached by several students in the schools where she had given her talks about choosing productive paths in life. Both male and female students commented on the lack of a male figure in their own lives and how it had impacted them. Faith sympathized, but, on reflection, she realized she now had something to say on the topic. She now felt that a father figure need not be the one who donated sperm. Mason Jeffries proved that truth, despite the lost years.

She continued with her letter text while Vilma wrote on the paper pad by her side.

The kitchen was quiet.

The dogs were asleep.

The house was silent.

It was as if the whole world was blanketed in snow and all normal activity was suspended.

And yet, two minds were active in the silence.

Vilma had dreams for the house she and Andy would share. She decided to consult the list of everything she might desire in their home. She had gone over it so often that she had no trouble recalling the details.

Now she wanted to apply some serious practical thinking. She would attempt to review her list by imagining what Andy would say about it. If she could come up with a reasonable compromise, it would make the whole project more acceptable to him and thus speed it along.

After his rescue of her yesterday, she did not want to challenge his patience in this matter. She saw the house was not uppermost in his mind and this she accepted.

The initial list was huge.

It contained such items as:

- an extra bedroom for the dogs
- a luxurious ensuite washroom
- large windows to capture the view
- a handsome front porch
- a wooden deck for privacy
- a large kitchen
- a laundry room
- a walk-in closet for her clothes
- a fenced garden
- a garage for her car
- and a paved path between the house and the barn

She was particularly pleased with the last two items as she felt they reflected her desire to be practical.

She paused at this point and realized she must think about costs. The truth was, Vilma Smith had no clue as to the cost of the simplest building or house feature. She had always had men around to worry about the money and those men had encouraged her to dream big.

After the extension to the barn was completed, there would not be much money left for the house. Andy had explained about the small sleeping area he planned for himself until the work was done. She dreaded having to share that accommodation with him as it sounded so primitive. It was enough to have seen what he considered adequate when he lived in the broken-down farmhouse. His idea of adequate was not hers.

She sighed and Astrid looked up briefly to see what she needed. It looked like it would be necessary to remain here at Harmony House much longer than she would prefer. There was no point in pretending she would be happy roughing it with Andy in the barn extension.

As she looked around at the fittings of the kitchen in which she sat, she realized staying on was not going to be a punishment. Everything here was immaculate, designed for comfort and fully climate controlled. Her bedroom was spacious and exactly as she wanted. She doubted it would suit Andy's style if, in fact, he had such a thing as a style.

Folding the list, and placing it in her pocket, she rose and returned to her room. There was a lot more thinking to do before she could tackle this topic of discussion.

To her surprise, the dogs remained with Faith.

She did not call them to her side as she walked slowly along the hall to her room. She needed solitude to consider the future and another short nap would help.

CHAPTER 6

When the mail was delivered the next day, Hilary knew the worst of the storm was over.

She spread the pile on the top of the table in the front entrance and immediately discarded, into a bin under the table, all the useless detritus of advertising materials, piling the rest into neat bundles with the recipient's name clearly visible on the top item.

She noticed there were three letters for Vilma and decided to take these upstairs. It was a good excuse to see how Vilma was faring today. Andy had called partway through the morning to ask her to keep an eye on Vilma for him.

"I'll be gone till late. She slept well last night but she mustn't do too much, too fast. She's had a big shock. Try to get her to rest. I had a word with Faith when I drove her to school today. She'll take the dogs out for their evening run and I'll bring back food for the three of us.

Hilary, I want you to know how much I appreciate your kindness in allowing me to camp out with Vilma.

You could easily object and you would be within your rights to do so."

She had interrupted him swiftly.

"Andy Patterson, you are one of the family here at Harmony House. Don't you dare say another word about that. Your presence is a comfort and help to all of us. I'll do what you advise for Vilma and we will see you later.

Have a safe day."

A gentle tap on Vilma's door produced a firm, "Please come in!"

Vilma was seated by the window. She was warmly dressed with hair brushed and a minimum of make-up applied.

Not that she needs it, thought Hilary. *This woman would look good wrapped in a plastic bag. The miracle is that she does not realize how attractive she really is. It's not all about the exterior either. She is a truly good human.*

Hilary popped her head around the door to give her report. She did not want to interrupt.

"I am bringing your mail, Vilma. Andy called and told me to check in on you. He will bring food for both of you and for Faith on his way home. Faith will take care of the dogs tonight so you can get extra rest."

"Come in please, Hilary. I need to talk to you. Sit here beside me. Thank you for the mail delivery.

It seems we don't see much of each other lately, for one reason or another. If you can spare a couple of minutes I would like to ask how you feel about Andy being here so often."

"Well, my dear, I feel as if you two are on the same wavelength. Andy said something similar earlier today. I'll repeat what I said to him then. He is welcome. All of us appreciate his situation.

You know, Vilma, we have watched you two getting closer for many months now and we feel quite delighted at how things have worked out for you. Yes, this is a difficult patch, but things will improve before long."

Vilma reached out for Hilary's hand and gave it a friendly squeeze.

"That's just it, Hilary. You are most kind but we

may be imposing on your generosity longer than expected. Andy's latest plan is to build onto the barn first, so his new business can get up and running.

He will do most of the work himself and with his pals until the insurance money comes through.

There is one piece of good news. I am making plans to take Andy away to Jamaica for a week in February."

"Now, that *is* good news. After the recent scare, both of you could do with a break. Andy works too hard. He must not exhaust himself with all these projects added to his work schedule."

"I am glad you agree, Hilary. He does worry about money and I have had an idea to help out with that. I am choosing a couple to occupy the second beach house in Jamaica. This will help with my costs but I have another motive for doing it. If this couple is congenial, I am thinking of offering them my room at Harmony House when I vacate it."

There was an audible intake of breath from Hilary.

What on earth is she thinking?

"Wait! Let me explain. This won't happen for some time, as I explained already, but I want to save you and Mavis the bother of finding a new candidate for my accommodations. I will retain my financial share in the co-housing unit until I am satisfied the new occupants are acceptable to everyone. They will pay only the monthly expenses while they are here."

Hilary was blinking rapidly as she attempted to assimilate this information.

"But where will you find these people, and how do you know they will fit in here?"

"I have been communicating with other co-housing projects in Canada to see if there are people who might want to move here on a trial basis. I whittled down the list to three and I believe there could be a response in one of these envelopes.

One couple shares an apartment in Manitoba and want to be closer to a family member who will be in hospital for treatment at London Health Sciences Centre. Another couple is from the East Coast and wish to escape from the horrible stormy weather they have had there in recent years. A third candidate.............."

"Wait a minute, Vilma! This is something quite different from our original premise. I can't approve or disapprove of this idea without consulting everyone else. I do appreciate your attempt to save us trouble in filling your place here, but there are legal implications in these choices. For a start, the idea was to have one person per bedroom, not two. I understand about Andy, of course but I just can't approve that change on my own."

"I do see that, Hilary. In some ways it is asking a lot, but if you look back at the changes that have occurred already the original plan of six women was altered significantly before we were very far into the process."

Both thought of the transition Faith had brought and both realized how quickly those changes had been absorbed. There was also the matter of Andy Patterson. There was no question that he was an asset to the co-housing plan. Hilary could not deny it.

"Well, Vilma, I suggest this matter be tabled on Sunday at our regular dinner meeting. I'll have a word with as many as I can find to give them a 'heads up' about the importance of attending.

In the meantime, please keep me up to date with your decisions. What you do about the Jamaica holiday is, of course, a separate item."

When Hilary had gone, presumably to talk to Mavis, Vilma opened the letters that were waiting on the table in front of her.

The first was a bank letter with an offer of added privileges for her chequing account. She set it aside with a rueful smile. She might soon need the advantages on offer.

The second was from her financial advisor requesting a meeting to discuss her tax situation.

Financial decisions are converging on me and I need to deal with all of this very soon.

She opened up the third letter with some trepidation, but found a very pleasant reply from the Manitoba couple. They were cousins, called Amanda Lennox and Braden Santiago who were originally from South America. Amanda's mother, Braden's aunt, was about to begin radiation therapy for liver cancer and the two wanted to be close for support during the three months of her treatment.

We both loved the idea of Harmony House and, as we are already adjusted to this style of living, it seems like a good match for us. Your lovely Jamaican holiday idea is a super bonus, from our perspective, and would give us a chance to get to know you better.

You may have a number of candidates in mind for this experiment, Ms. Smith, but we want you to know we are ready and eager to be considered among them.

Vilma put the letter down and took a deep breath. Things were moving fast. Amanda and Braden sounded like excellent candidates but she must wait to see if more letters or emails arrived.

Nothing could be decided until the results of Sunday's house meeting had been digested.

~

On Sunday, Andy was meeting with three of his team to look over the building specs for the barn extension. He warned them it was not a pleasant venue as the limited heating was restricted to a corner of the actual barn area and there were not facilities nearby for food.

As a result, the guys arrived with a supply of hot Italian food from Dolcetto's restaurant on Colonel Talbot Road and a six pack of beer to keep the workers hydrated.

It was not long before Andy realized how vital his helpers' advice would be. He had drawn up a rough plan but Brady quickly pointed out a major flaw that would have cost him hundreds of dollars to amend later in the process.

Frank quickly had his sleeves rolled up and a wheelbarrow-load of stones from the old farmhouse's foundations set out to show the dimensions of the proposed extension so they could walk round the space and discuss what might work there.

Joe liked the idea of enclosing an open area with a drystone wall and he said his brother-in-law was an expert at walls and would donate his labour in exchange for a couple of beers one weekend when the weather was warmer.

Andy happily agreed to the proposed changes when they asked him about his overall plan and they consolidated it all into a temporary second storey living space that would convert to an office with the housing for dogs down below. The extension would have links to the barn to make moving back and forth simpler and the whole project must have security and technology incorporated so, when the new house was built, Andy could keep an eye on his canine boarders from a distance.

He was staggered at how valuable the input of these men had been. New sets of eyes had transformed his plan into a more practical and less expensive form. *And*, it had all happened in the space of a few hours.

It was another important stage on his way to recovery. These guys were old friends and good buddies. He no longer needed to do everything on his own.

His relief was palpable.

He was not alone. He had never been alone, except by choice.

He could not wait to get back to Harmony House to share the new plans with Vilma but when he approached the house in the early evening, he heard the sound of dogs barking and soon found Faith outside in charge of Astrid and Oscar. Faith seemed to have the dogs under control and he was pleased to see this.

She signalled to him to come over to her by the woods where he was eagerly greeted by the dogs, who immediately presumed they were off to explore again.

"Pay no attention to them, Andy. They've been out with me for thirty minutes already.

I've been waiting to see you to tell you what's going on inside."

"What do you mean, Faith? Is Vilma all right?"

"I hope so. She's being grilled about this replacement residents idea. It started right after dinner and I excused myself fast when I saw what was happening."

"Are you saying there's going to be trouble about this? Vilma is only trying to be helpful."

"I don't know. It sounded complicated to me and I'm in no position to offer my opinion. I don't even contribute to my place here."

"That applies to me too, Faith. We are both very fortunate to have been accepted by these good people.

I'm sure it will worked out to everyone's satisfaction in the end. Don't you worry!

Your nose is turning blue, my girl! Let's get these two inside and I'll make coffee and hot chocolate for us in Vilma's room once the dogs are fed."

Andy was attempting to be positive for Faith's sake but inwardly he was very nervous about the situation. He appreciated he was asking a great deal of Vilma. Her settled life in Harmony House had been totally disrupted by his arrival here. He could not know how much pressure it would take for her to decide to abandon his sketchy plans for their future and prefer to continue in the comfortable setting she had claimed as her own.

The high spirits he felt after spending time on the farm property with the guys, dissipated in a cloud of doubt. He knew how much Vilma respected the five women to whom she had become close. He could never insist on removing her from her place, a place in which she had invested a considerable amount of her money. He could not match that investment. The choice was all hers. It must be that way.

He nibbled on a thumb nail as Faith rinsed out their cups and left, with the excuse of homework to complete. The room grew silent other than for the intermittent snores of Oscar.

He sat near the window, looking out on the winter darkness, and waited impatiently for his fate to be decided.

~

"Why are you sitting in the dark, Andy?

Have you had anything to eat? Let me put on the lights and we can talk."

Her voice sounded brighter than he expected and she looked recovered from her recent ordeal.

His hopes began to rise again.

"I see you made coffee. Please pour me a cup. I am parched with talking for the last hour."

He jumped up; glad to have something useful to do.

Vilma greeted the dogs and plopped down on top of her bed, patting the space beside her so he would join her with the coffee mugs.

She did not make him wait any longer. It was clear from his face that Faith had filled him in on the Sunday supper discussion.

"Andy, it's OK! We had a good airing of opinions both positive and negative. In the end, my idea was accepted. The most conciliatory suggestion came from Mavis who confessed she was uncomfortable with her huge tower room and offered to exchange hers with mine to better accommodate two women."

"What? How does that work? I can't predict how much of the building work will be completed when we come home at the start of March. Where will you go then, Vilma?"

"I don't know, Andy.

Maybe I'll bunk in with Hilary. We'll see!

It all depends on how compatible we are with the cousins from Manitoba. I got their letter today and I think they will be my choice for Jamaica.

It's not worth worrying about it all yet.

One step at a time.

Now snuggle down and tell me about *your* day."

CHAPTER 7

It was the frequent and natural conclusion to the Sunday meal for Hilary to nudge Mavis and lead her along the hall to her tower room after the kitchen dishes were cleared up. She waited until the double door firmly closed behind them before she began.

"What on earth were you thinking, Mavis? The lower tower room is yours by rights. Why should you give it up to strangers?"

"Now Hilary, you know I was not happy claiming such a huge space for myself. I always intended to offer it to one of the others, if the occasion arose. In any case, it's likely to be temporary. The dogs should stay with me in Vilma's room where they are most comfortable for the week

Vilma and Andy are away. After that we don't know what will happen."

"Never mind the dogs. What about your Marble? How will she feel about being displaced?"

"Oh, Marble spends most of the day sleeping under the piano in Faith's room. She'll follow me wherever I go to sleep and eat."

"But! But!"

"Hilary Dempster, my decision does not mean you will ever be required to give up this room of yours. So don't be concerned about that. A similar situation requiring changes might have arisen at any time although I did not expect it to happen so soon. With the range in ages of our original group, there was always the chance that someone would want to move out. We need to be flexible. Vilma and Andy are a good couple and I believe they will be happy together. That is the fact we must deal with now."

Hilary began to pace around the room in an attempt to absorb her friend's point of view.

"Mavis, you are a never-ending source of amazement to me. I don't know how you can accept this so easily. I thought we were over the first adjustments and things would move ahead in a more predictable way from here on."

"Really? You think I am the only one who is amazing?

You are more flexible than you realize, my dear.

Remember the sudden arrival of Faith? You took on that challenge pretty fast as I recall, and I think you enjoyed the way the girl added youth and vitality to all of us. She allowed Honor to become a more complete person for one thing.

Change is inevitable in any sphere of life these days."

"You are conveniently forgetting the disruption that girl brought to us initially, and also there's the incident with the top of the tower room more recently. We may not be out of the woods with that young lady yet."

"True! But what happens if Honor and Faith decide to go live in Kingston?

What if Jannice gets more attached to that Mitchell who is writing about her family?

What if Eve becomes famous for her paintings and goes off with an artist?"

"Stop! Mavis you are scaring me. Do you really think these things could happen? I hate the idea of our lovely group of women being shattered like that. I expected our idea of mutual support would last until we are both carried out of here feet first. I just don't see how we could replace our friends. It changes everything I believed about our co-housing project.

Were we wrong to try this experiment?"

Mavis patted her friend's shoulder and attempted to allay her fears.

"Not at all, Hilary! It's a brilliant idea and it has worked very well on the whole. We have already proved our adaptability. We chose generous people to live with us and I know we can survive any changes that may come in time. We have a superb house here and it is home now. A home we could never have dreamed of when we went through the awful years of losing our life partners."

Hilary could not deny the truth of what she was hearing.

Back then, with Mavis in her house on one side of town, and Hilary far away in Camden Corners, they were settling into a dark and depressing period relieved only by phone calls in which they commiserated with their fates as newly-single women with fewer choices in life. The decision to attempt a co-housing project had brought them both closer than ever and given them something positive to focus on.

Of course, the resulting events had made their lives better.

She shook off her worries and concentrated on Mavis again.

"At this very moment, Mavis my dear, I am

thinking of that list you have in your room. You know, the one you showed me with the five best indicators for a happy life? Are you still undecided about the last one, the unusual word, 'conscientousness'?"

Mavis nodded. She could not see where this was leading. Hilary seemed to have changed direction rather suddenly.

"Well, I did look up the word for you and I am happy to tell you it suits you perfectly. It describes a person with a strong moral sense, a scrupulous attention to honesty and a deep, intuitive power of doing the right thing."

"Hilary! Did you memorize that definition?"

"I had to. It was quite complex, but it is *you*, Mavis. I will try never to doubt your instincts again.

My best decision was to partner with you in all things. I defer to your superior judgement."

Mavis laughed out loud and with the cheerful sound all tension in the room dissolved.

Oh, Hilary Dempster! That is a beautiful compliment. I take it with a grain of salt, however. The important thing is that we function well as a team. That will not change as long as we have our health and strength and, quite possibly, long after that!"

Laughter led to happy tears and on to a soothing cup of tea.

Sunday evening in Hilary's tower room ended amicably with all fears assuaged, for the time being.

~

Faith was happy to relinquish the dogs to Andy and return to her room. Homework was the excuse she used, but her real intention was to get started on the vlog letter.

She had discussed this idea with Jolene during lunch in the Library at school. Since Faith was now famous at Saunders owing to her high profile among both staff and students, she had gained the privilege of eating and talking with her friend in a quiet corner, without interruption. Often their conversation was about other matters than the next scheduled talk about life choices, but the librarians smiled at them and gave them a wide berth, as long as things did not get too raucous and they cleared away all signs of eating before they left.

Jolene was approving of the 'Dear Dad' letter.

"It fits in with what you did before and oh boy did that work! The responses are still coming in.

It's hard for me to believe how many kids' lives are different from the standard pattern of mom, dad and 2.1 children. It adds up to a heap of human sorrow out there.

You gave them a voice, Faith. I say go for it."

Now that everyone at Harmony House knew what she had done online, it was no longer necessary to make the difficult and dangerous climb up to the top of the tower. She thought of that period in her life as a time when she was young and foolish. Now she felt as if she had grown up so much that she sometimes had trouble recognizing herself in the mirror.

She settled in front of her laptop in her room, after making sure there would be nothing in the background to identify her location. The last thing she wanted was for a procession of teenage fans to arrive at Harmony House looking for her. Even the kids at school were unaware of her address since she arrived and left on the bus most days.

The J.J. gang had been warned to say nothing about her living situation. It was enough that the world knew about her personal and private stuff. She did not intend to give away anything more after this final entry.

She tried to write down her feelings about the missing father situation but it sounded too formal on paper. She would just 'wing it' and erase the post if she did not like the result.

Gone was the dark hoodie. She had nothing to hide any more.

Hi There YouTubers!

This is Faith, also known as J.J., telling you about a letter that will never be written, or ever sent.

It's heading would be, 'Letter to the Father I Never Knew'.

I guess it's more accurate to call you my biological father. You are a complete unknown to me. An invisible presence I never even wondered about until much later. As a child, it was just me and Mom. You were not in the picture at all. I did not miss you.

Not when Mom cried at night. Not when there was no food left. Not when Mom went out alone and I was afraid. Not when she started to take the stuff that left her helpless for hours on end.

You see I did not know about you. I thought I did, because there was another guy, a substitute dad, who hung around for a few years early on when things were mostly OK. I hardly remembered him. He took off when Mom's behaviour got out of hand. After that, there was a lot of moving around and scary times when we were jumping just ahead of the authorities.

You could call it living on the edge. On the edge of disaster that is. The worst part was feeling so alone with

*no one to ask for help when I did not know what to do
next. I could have used a real father then. Many times.*

*The good news is that I survived . Mom did not. Too
much worry and abuse of many kinds wore her right
down and she was gone. Gone, as in dead. Not gone, as in
a dad who donated his sperm and disappeared from view
without knowing there had been results.*

*I was one of the lucky ones. My life finally took a turn
for the better. Along the way in foster homes, I learned
how lucky I was to be found by people who care. Women
who opened their hearts and home to a crazy teen and
showed her how to be a human being with hopes and
dreams.*

*I found, in this home, an aunt I knew nothing of, and
who did not know about me either. We are working out
our relationship. She filled in some of the background
story for me.*

*I finally found friends my own age at school.
Friends whose lives had been the exact opposite of
mine. At first, I felt like an alien visiting friends in a
peaceful home with two parents, a brother, a regular
routine and regular meals. Thanks to Jo, I learned how
to behave in that setting although it was very hard
at first.*

*Yes, it's hard with no father, but as it turns out, I
really managed quite well without you. I guess I learned a
few good survival skills along the way.*

I also found the guy who took your place at the beginning and he has folded me into his family.

I now have everything I need.

I made it.

Don't worry I won't be looking for you. Like other deadbeat dads in the world, you are anonymous and safe.

I kinda hope you wonder, once in a while, about the unhappy young girl you knocked up long ago.

Or else, since you had no conscience then, or now, I'll just continue to forget you completely.

After all, you don't deserve to be remembered.

Goodbye forever.

Over and out from J.J.

She watched the entry over once and sent it quickly before she could change her mind. Then she went outside and walked along the covered porch thinking and wondering.

She hoped that, somewhere in the great unknown of the afterlife, her Mom was aware of how well things had worked out for her daughter.

She saw a gleam of light stretching across the snow and figured out it must come from the lantern Andy had placed in the tiny tower-top room. It was like a beacon of hope in the darkness.

The light shone toward Louise and Dennis

Ridley's home. Faith took it as a sign, a message for her.

If the Ridleys were able to adopt a child, as Mavis believed they would, Faith Jeffries promised to help that child in any way she could. It was a kind of payback; a pay-it-forward for all the luck she had received in her life.

With a deep feeling of peace in her heart, she returned to Harmony House and soon fell fast asleep.

CHAPTER 8

The month of February seemed to race along at top speed to the residents of Harmony House.

After the deep freeze of January weather, even a slight improvement in the temperature brought more vitality to everyone.

Honor and Mavis continued their yoga sessions and Hilary joined them once. After only a few minutes she declared her long body was never meant to bend and twist in that fashion and she would content herself with walking up and down stairs instead of using the elevator. Now that her routine of visiting and driving pensioners had resumed, she was often out of the house for hours at a time.

"That is quite enough exercise for me, ladies. I admire your ambition, and your flexibility."

Mavis noted the word 'flexibility' and thought it was going to be a quality the entire household would need in the coming weeks. Vilma and Andy were heading off to Jamaica very soon and there they would meet with the couple from Manitoba for the first time. If the cousins proved to be compatible, Vilma intended to invite them to join the Harmony House family permanently, taking up her space as soon as the new house was finished at Andy's farm location.

Although Mavis had great faith in Vilma's good judgement, she was apprehensive about the choice of a couple to replace one person. The financial implications of that decision had not yet been fully determined. Hilary insisted there was enough going on, at the present time, without borrowing trouble from the future; a future that might not develop as everyone was expecting.

"Think about it Mavis. If the new couple proves to be unsatisfactory in some way, the entire idea is moot. Vilma may decide to retain her options with us for some years yet, until Andy's business is operating with a profit. We just don't know, so why worry?"

It seemed eminently sensible at the time of their

conversation, but Mavis could sense change rumbling in the house and not all of it was about the weather.

Eve had recently made a good friend of one of the women in her Byron Art club. Cheryl had a condo in the states and she invited Eve to join her for a week or two to visit the museum in Santa Fe dedicated to the amazing flower studies and other art of Georgia O'Keefe. Mavis was encouraging Eve to do this and to take her painting supplies with her. It would be a break from winter in Ontario and could give her ideas for future work.

Jannice had been working away quietly since her visit to Quebec City at Christmas but she was still in touch with Mitchell Delaney and planning a visit from him in the spring. With the television series, Alias Grace, giving renewed attention to the plight of poor Irish immigrants in nineteenth–century Upper Canada, Mitchell wanted to research the locations in Toronto and area where some of the actual incidents of the Grace Marks story took place. Jannice had agreed to accompany him.

That makes three rooms vacant temporarily, for one reason or another.

Her mind now drifted toward Faith and her aunt.

Honor was not likely to be going anywhere soon. She was dedicated to her business concerns and conscious of making enough money to justify her niece's occupation of a space in Harmony House.

Faith, however, was another matter altogether. Honor had shared with Mavis and Hilary her delight at the attention sixteen-year-old Faith had garnered on YouTube.

"I know she's still very young but she is getting offers of scholarships already. She's in line for community awards that come with monetary prizes and if she can maintain her present academic success she may be able to apply to a community college or university anywhere in Canada, even before she has completed high school."

Honor gave due praise to both Hilary and Mavis for their help and support of Faith.

"I will never be able to thank you two ladies enough for taking her in and teaching both of us how to become family to each other."

Honor mentioned nothing specific, but it was in the back of Mavis's mind that Faith's extended family now included the Kingston Jeffries. There was really nothing to prevent Honor from following her niece to Kingston, if that was her decision.

Five possibly-vacant rooms at Harmony House! Good grief!

Vilma's idea of permitting short-term exchanges in their rooms was becoming more of a viable notion. It would not add to the financial benefits of the current residents, but it was something of a charitable move as in the case of the cousins whose mother and aunt was going to be in hospital in London.

She thought about what it would be like to have different people coming and going in their space and, to her surprise, she found it was interesting to realize how many other lives they could touch in this way. It was like a network of friends and acquaintances stretching out beyond their own borders and adding options to their future. She thought of herself and Hilary as the doorkeepers welcoming new people into their environment for short periods, but it was always possible that the two of them could also take advantage of the opportunity to experience new places. She had always had a secret dream of visiting Vancouver and seeing the snow-topped mountains towering over the city by the sea.

After all, it would be an inexpensive way to travel.

If it ever came to pass?

If the inevitable difficulties could be overcome?

If.

It was nice to dream, especially in mid-winter, but the compatibility factor was the unknown.

One incident of disruption or damage caused by the strangers in their midst would sour the entire enterprise.

She concluded it was just as well that Vilma and Andy were spending a whole week with the cousins.

If that couple were not suitable candidates to occupy space in Harmony House, Vilma Smith would know and her plan would change.

As had been said before........time would tell. It was not worth worrying over much about it all right now.

~

Vilma found herself totally giddy over the prospect of a week in Jamaica with Andy.

Their time together had been limited in the last two months owing to the work on the barn extension. To save money, Andy was doing as much of the labour as the weather and his skills allowed. On the nights when he chose to come to Harmony House, he often arrived late, ate quickly, and fell asleep before Vilma emerged from the washroom. She loved seeing him enjoying the warmth and comfort she supplied. It was a hard road he had chosen to follow, but his pride remained intact as long as he was working toward his goal of providing for them.

There had been conversations about the wisdom of taking time away for a holiday. She knew he was worried about the deadline for opening the dog training business. Advertising had already been circulated to make dog owners aware of the new facility. Andy wanted to be sure to be ready for the proposed opening date. A website was up and working, thanks to the expertise of one of Andy's former team members. Brady agreed to supervise that while they were away.

Vilma filled in the time by working with Faith on dog routines, revising and simplifying her new home plans and keeping communication going with Amanda and Braden. This was done mostly by email as the cousins were working on some project that took them out of their co-housing unit for several hours a day.

Amanda was the best writer of the pair and Vilma enjoyed her folksy style although there was not much about the more personal stuff related to age and preferences. Vilma assumed all of that would become clear once they met in person. She had discussed the travel arrangements to co-ordinate from two different departure airports. She and Andy would have one night on their own before the cousins arrived. Every time she thought about the paradise location in their separate villa with the stars burning overhead, a shiver of delight ran through her.

It was the beginning of a new part of their lives together. They would finally have the chance to concentrate fully on each other.

She could hardly wait.

CHAPTER 9

The plane journey from Canada to Jamaica was exactly the transition Vilma needed.

She was exhilarated as each hour passed and brought her nearer to the island. Andy was sleeping by her side, which was not a surprise. She knew how many hours he had put in on the barn extension during the week prior to their departure from London. She had not visited the site lately as he assured her it was a mess of mud and stones, better left alone until more work had been finished. He did have one piece of good news, shown to her in a photograph. The name 'Patterson' was now painted in bold letters across the side of the barn facing the laneway. It would draw attention as far away as the access road from town.

Andy said there were already a number of enquiries online about dog training programs. It looked as if customers needed help with puppy training rather than the show work he had hoped for, but it would be necessary to start small and work up to the major stuff.

Vilma listened and agreed with everything he said. She planned to abolish all work discussions in Jamaica.

This week was to be a complete change from everything they left behind them in Canada.

They collected their cases at the airport and walked out into tropical warmth. Vilma watched as Andy's shoulders relaxed followed by his intaken breath and his eyes traversing the waving palm trees and vivid plants. She knew the magic would work on him as it always did for her.

The mini-bus ride to their destination passed swiftly while Vilma answered Andy's questions about everything he saw on the way. When they drew into the parking spot on the roadside, he asked where the buildings were.

Vilma signalled to him to follow her as she wound down the narrow pathway through the foliage until they reached the beach.

At this point all thoughts of buildings vanished as Andy was instantly enraptured by the pristine sandy beach bordered by crystal waves lapping on the shoreline in the crescent-shaped cove. He immediately bent down to remove his shoes then grabbed Vilma's hand and walked along the water's edge just taking it all in.

There were no more questions. He could see everything necessary for himself.

When they reached the palm- fringed hut on the far side of the crescent, Leon emerged to greet Vilma and handed the couple tall drinks liberally festooned with straws and slices of fruit.

"Welcome back, Vilma Smith! You brought beautiful sunshine with you as always. Your luggage is being delivered as we speak and the villa is ready for you. I'll send lunch in a few minutes but for now enjoy the view please."

Vilma introduced Andy as her special guest and she and Leon exchanged information about her previous year's guests while Andy sipped and stared around him. He could now detect the villas partly hidden among the thick bank of greenery on the slope. There were only a few of these residences to be seen. He realized this was a very exclusive resort for a few, very rich travellers. It was typical of Vilma to underplay the cost factor but, for once, he decided to let all the financial stuff go in favour of accepting this generous gift in the spirit in which it was intended.

He could already sense some of the tension his body and mind had been carrying for so long, floating away from him in the soft breeze from the aquamarine sea. This was truly paradise. He decided it would be churlish to do anything other than absorb it and enjoy it with all his heart.

He removed his shirt and felt the sun on his skin.

Vilma watched and smiled. The island magic was at work on him. All would be well.

Their first night together in the cottage was all that Vilma had hoped for. Andy could hardly believe how beautiful the sunset was. He sat on the deck and watched the stars appear overhead and it seemed as if the setting loosened his tongue. He spoke of holidays he had taken with his wife and stated nothing they had ever seen would compare to the privacy and splendour of this place.

As Andy had never mentioned his ex-wife before this moment, Vilma was at first shocked, then pleased to know there would be no further secrets between them. He knew about her two marriages. The way ahead was now clear.

They shared a bottle of rich red wine and fell into the luxurious bed together, with the shutters open to the cool breeze and only the sound of waves to lull them to sleep.

~

Everything changed in mid-afternoon of the following day.

Vilma stayed in the cottage after inspecting the smaller, walkway-linked villa that was to accommodate the cousins from Manitoba. She wanted to be on hand to welcome them as soon as they arrived at the resort.

She sent Andy for a walk along the beach to meet some of the residents whose padded deck chairs were already arranged on the sand under large sun umbrellas. She made Andy apply protective sun lotion and gave him a wide-brimmed sun hat from her case. He looked the part with his broad shoulders and strong legs and she knew he would fit in perfectly.

As soon as she heard the sound of excited voices she went to the end of the pathway to meet her guests. She first saw two sets of legs approaching but it was not until the rest of the bodies appeared that she realized Amanda and Braden were not as she had expected.

Only one of the couple was a female. The other was quite definitely male. Both cousins had skin the colour of chestnuts and luxurious jet black hair. Amanda was the talkative one. She swept back her hair in one hand and stretched out the other with a big smile that revealed the most perfect white teeth imaginable.

"You must be Vilma Smith. Thank you so much for arranging this. The place is *absolutely gorgeous*, such a contrast to snowy, freezing Manitoba. I said to Braden we are so lucky to be chosen to come here and meet you. I never thought we would be so fortunate when I sent out the first email to you. We've been so worried about Mama going to London all by herself but we could not see a way to afford the accommodation even with all the hospital did to make it work. This holiday is just what we need before the hard stuff of helping her through the treatment. We mean to be the best guests ever, Vilma, in hopes you will choose us to live in your Harmony House for a time. Right Braden?"

Braden had shaken Vilma's hand but he had not yet spoken one word. With a voluble cousin like Amanda, Vilma guessed there was not much need for him to speak.

In an attempt to give herself a few moments to disguise her shock, Vilma led them up the short path to the villas and pointed out their own private accommodation with the twin beds, kitchen area and deck.

"I'll leave you two to get settled. Your luggage will arrive shortly. Come over to the other villa when you are ready and we'll have a good chat."

She smiled, what she hoped was a genuine smile, and scuttled off to her bedroom. She needed time to reset her expectations.

Would Mavis and Hilary accept a male resident? Of course, they both loved Andy but his introduction had been slow to develop over years now. What would they say to a strange man suddenly arriving in their midst?

Perhaps it all depended on Amanda. She composed her face. The next few minutes would be crucial. She was glad Andy was otherwise occupied on the beach.

Braden was the first to arrive and she heard his voice at last. It had the same pleasant lilting tone as Amanda's.

"Sorry! Mandy is unpacking and fussing around. She sent me ahead. I imagine you have questions?"

Vilma set out fresh lime drinks and settled down

beside him on the deck. She wondered how to start without appearing rude.

"Well, tell me a bit about the two of you?"

"I am happy to do that. I saw you were surprised when we arrived. We are an unusual pair, more like brother and sister than cousins, I suppose. Our family came to Canada from the British Virgin Islands via Colombia and Venezuela. I lost my mother long ago and Amanda's mother took me in right away. I owe everything to her. That's why we are so grateful for your offer of accommodation. There are only we three left now so this time is precious to us. Amanda's father was a very smart man with multi language skills that earned him a place in a university. He worked hard until the day he died and left us with enough money to live in a co-housing unit. We both work as web designers with clients across the world but we have a distaste for hotels and such bland accommodations. We had a big family group once upon a time. Some emigrated to other countries along the way. We need to be together and with others around. It's what we are used to. It's where we feel most comfortable, so co-housing meets our needs perfectly.

I hope we can make use of this time together. You have chosen a magnificent spot in which to relax. It will be good to get to know you better, Vilma Smith."

He raised his glass in a salute. Vilma had listened to his brief biographical explanation but her attention was split between his words and his appearance. He was probably the most handsome man she had ever seen, outside of a movie theatre. His shock of shining black hair fell over a high forehead where thick and expressive eyebrows shaded his dark eyes. He had the fan-shaped eyelashes girls always crave and his skin was even-coloured and gleaming with health. She put his age at about thirty-five although it was hard to tell. She could not avoid the conclusion that he and Amanda looked so much more at home in this tropical paradise than did she and Andy with their pale northern complexions.

Amanda soon arrived wearing a pair of flowered shorts with an overskirt that suited her similar gorgeous skin and hair to perfection. She had a swimsuit underneath. She was burbling over with praise of their accommodations and of how she was looking forward to this holiday in the sun.

"Manitoba has been good to us but we are basically sun-bunnies, if you don't mind the description, Vilma. We always plan a holiday from winter, but we have never been to a secluded spot like this one.

You have chosen well. Braden and me want to ask you if we can pay for meals for all four of us? The payment you asked for this private villa was not nearly enough. This place is *really special*! Right, Braden?"

"We will discuss that later when Andy arrives. He's on the beach. Would you like to swim now, Amanda? You too, Braden?"

"Absolutely! I can't wait. Braden brought snorkeling gear. He loves the water."

They went off together down the wooden track and ran like children straight into the waves, hand in hand.

Vilma saw Andy watching as he strode along the beach toward their villa with a tray of fruit snacks in his hands. As most of the resort's residents were older people it was unusual to see such youthful high spirits in the late afternoon when it was customary for naps to be enjoyed before the evening meal service.

Vilma realized she had a lot to share with Andy and, also, that this week was not likely to be quite what she had expected.

~

As the days went by, Vilma grew more and more pleased with their companions. They were eager to see as much of the island as possible and since Andy agreed with this plan, they were off in taxis to explore for a part of each day. Their lunch was often eaten on a raised patio with an ocean view, featuring a selection of fresh fish caught that morning. Bernard and Amanda were excellent companions with tales of their past lives and present Canadian holiday adventures that enlivened every conversation.

They visited Dunn's Falls and went out on glass-bottomed boats to see the colourful tropical fish darting in the clear sea waters. They rode on horses into the Blue Mountains and brought back coffee and spices. One evening they chartered a sailing ship and had supper while sailing along the shore past hotels and resorts that seemed crassly modern compared to their own secluded, low-key residence at Pirate Cove.

Andy and Braden immediately bonded over discussions related to his business and the new website. It was not long before Braden gave him several good ideas for promoting his skills and attracting clients.

The two men huddled together after walks along

the beach while Amanda and Vilma talked freely about love and life and the future.

Vilma gave her a review of the whole Harmony House project, emphasizing the important roles of Hilary and Mavis.

"Really, it has grown and changed organically as time went on but there were always unexpected developments along the way."

"I can understand that. Our present location is where we have lived for five years now. We have a two-bedroom apartment with kitchen facilities. It's in a good location on the edges of Winnipeg and we like the quiet around us. We each have a work station in our bedroom and share the common living room.

The others in the building are mostly younger folks but everyone keeps to themselves which suits us. There are times when special meals or events are shared and buses take us to local shopping when required. With the long winters we find it's cozy to stay indoors and get on with work but in summer we are out as much as possible with kayaking, running and sports of all kinds."

Vilma thought it was a good life for the cousins and she hoped they would fit in nicely at Harmony.

"I can't promise you two bedrooms, Amanda. Our suites are singles with ensuite washrooms, but the rooms are spacious and we have lots of outdoor and indoor spaces for your use. Of course, our winters are shorter than in Manitoba so you and Braden could take advantage of the outdoors more often than you are used to. London has many facilities for a mid-sized town, including a ski hill, and we are two hours by train or road from Toronto and close to two of the Great Lakes. It's even less than that time, to get to the tech hub of Waterloo."

"We researched the entire area before coming here, Vilma. It's a super location for us. We are really excited about the possibilities, but mainly that London has so much to offer in medical terms with several major hospitals. Mama is fortunate to be accepted for a new cancer treatment there."

Vilma thought there was one other person at Harmony House who would find these two very stimulating. Honor Pace might want to share her work area with them.

～

By the end of the week, Vilma realized that she had been somewhat distracted by the cousins and their life story. The precious private time with Andy had been cut short.

He was not complaining. He had enjoyed the

company of Braden and Amanda, company that often extended into the midnight hours as they watched the stars wheel around the sky and talked in the glow of golden lights outlining the pathways. Below, on the darkened beach, the waves were crested with luminosity.

The scene was magical and conversation often died away as they sat in comfort on the deck.

Amanda and Braden were up early, nonetheless. They invited Andy to try snorkeling while Vilma took a more leisurely approach to the day and admired the ambition of the trio with a large mug of coffee in hand.

∼

When the final day arrived, the mutual decision was to stay on the beach and relish their final hours in the glorious sunshine. They would travel together to the airport early the next morning and separate to different departure areas for their flights home.

Amanda assured Vilma they would stay in touch about her mother's move to London in the hopes it would coordinate with the work Andy had described on the farm and house.

"I can now say with confidence that you two would be welcomed at Harmony House. It's been great spending this time with you both. I hope it all works out for you and your mother, Mandy."

Suddenly finding herself alone and so close to Andy again in the plane, simply underlined her feeling of sacrificing her holiday hours in favour of the cousins and their concerns.

When she asked Andy how he felt about the holiday he replied that it was one of the best times of his life.

"They are a great couple and you looked after them very well, Vilma. I realize it was at the expense of our private time but in the long view, it will work out to our advantage if you can replace the gap you leave at Harmony House with such a friendly pair."

With that, he turned on the media viewer on the back of the seat in front and became immersed in the kind of trivial viewing that he never had the chance to do at the building site of the farm. She saw him relax physically and mentally and knew how taxing on him the winter weeks had been.

She could only hope that he was now feeling refreshed and energized enough to move the building project ahead at top speed.

CHAPTER 10

Andy brushed snow off his truck and drove out to the farm as soon as he took Vilma's luggage up to her room. He stopped for a minute to greet the dogs then blew Vilma a kiss as he ran downstairs to retrieve his winter coat.

Vilma went down to the lower level to find Honor and enquire how Faith had managed with the dogs in her absence.

"Hey there! Welcome home! The house has not been the same without you, Vilma. Sit down. I'll make you coffee and you can tell me all about your holiday."

Honor explained why the house seemed so quiet.

"No wonder you couldn't find anyone upstairs. Hilary is in town with her 'oldies' and Mavis is at the

Ridley home helping Louise set up a nursery for the children they are soon to be fostering.

Eve left a few days ago with her artist friend, Kylie, for a two-week vacation in Santa Fe.

I think Jannice is at work. She has erratic hours these days. Seniors are dropping like flies with influenza and pneumonia this winter. I thank God we are all healthy here at Harmony.

Oh, and Faith is at school, of course."

Vilma felt a passing pang of self-pity that all had gone on without her so smoothly during her absence.

Apparently, she had not been missed, other than by her dogs, and possibly Faith, who had taken over the responsibility for their care.

She shivered and Honor quickly took a wool shawl from her chair and placed it around Vilma's shoulders.

"You will feel the cold for a few days until you get adjusted. Can I warm up your coffee?"

Vilma snuggled into the shawl and took the cup between her hands for warmth as she spoke.

"So, tell me about Faith and the dogs. They are sleeping in my room now after a happy romp with me in which I got covered in dog hair. From what I saw they are in fine fettle."

"I kept a close eye on them from here, Vilma.

After what happened to you in the woods I was worried at first, but Faith is so good with Astrid and Oscar. They obey her commands due in part to the trick of having interesting treats in her jacket pocket! Andy also gave her a dog whistle.... one of those with supersonic sound that they can hear from anywhere? She used it once to my knowledge. That was when the dogs got too close to the frozen stream. The rest of the time, everything was good. She took them out first thing this morning before school."

"This is such good news, Honor. I am relieved and so grateful to Faith. It was quite a responsibility for a young girl to take on. I must say I am surprised."

Honor laughed right out loud.

"No more surprised than I am! If you had asked me a year ago if Faith could be left in charge of a pair of dogs I would have fainted from shock. She's an entirely different girl now. She's so mature and thoughtful. Much of that is due to everyone here at Harmony House, but her school experiences have helped enormously. Who would have thought her awful childhood could lead to such a deep desire to help other kids?"

"You have played a big part in Faith's success, Honor. Finding acceptance with a previously unknown relative gave her stability. Don't underestimate your influence."

"Thanks for saying that but I was a mess at the beginning. I floundered until Hilary and Mavis took charge."

"Those days are far behind us, Honor. We are all proud of Faith, and of you."

Honor blushed at this praise.

"Oh, I almost forgot! The response to Faith's recent 'Lost Father' letter has been astronomical. She's been asked to do more of the same to help teenagers. There are advertisers who are willing to sponsor her vlog time on a regular basis. Honestly, Vilma, there's no chance of her getting into any kind of trouble these days. She's too darn busy!"

Vilma was cheered by Honor's good news and decided to take the dogs out for a good long run in the Southwest baseball park that was often empty this time of year. She donned her long boots, lined gloves and warm hat. It was hard to get her coat on for the first time, but once attired in protection head to toe, she knew the tropical holiday was over and real life must now be resumed.

Cold weather or no cold weather.

Despite her good intentions, Vilma found the

outdoor weather to be insufferable. She cut the dog exercise short and made for the nearby Tim Hortons where she grabbed a hot coffee and a fruit explosion muffin, which she would carefully share with the dogs in tiny pieces.

Astrid and Oscar did not seem to be at all upset by this choice. They had run like mad things around and around the open space in the park making tracks in the deep snow that they continued to follow faithfully until they could run faster than ever on the packed surface. They returned to their mistress with huge grins that seemed to say, 'That was lovely, but now can we get back in the car?'

The daylight was fast disappearing when she left the Tim Horton parking lot and she headed home feeling more than a little tired and depressed.

Fortunately, Hilary and Mavis met her at the door to Harmony House with such a warm welcome that her spirits rose and she soon went to the kitchen with them to discover a lasagna with all the fixings waiting for her. Honor was slicing fresh bread and arranging portions of chocolate cream cake on plates for dessert.

When their first hunger was satisfied, conversation turned to the holiday in Jamaica. Mavis had enjoyed a week there the year before and she was eager to hear about the cousins.

"Did they fit in well with you and Andy at Pirate Cove?"

Vilma was uncertain how her news would be received, but she began to talk while crossing her fingers under the table for luck.

"Well, the cousins were a marvellous couple to share a holiday with. They are younger and more energetic but very personable and easy to get along with. They come from South America originally, and have travelled and lived in several countries on their way to Canada."

She paused and hesitated before continuing. She was deciding whether or not to make a joke of the next revelation but went ahead with her first impulse.

"There was one big surprise, however."

Everyone at the table stopped chewing and looked up. There was something unusual in Vilma's voice that drew their attention.

"You see, it turns out I made a mistake about them. I thought Braden was short for Bernadette or Bernice. The name was actually Braden, and he is a man."

Honor choked back a laugh. Vilma's face was a study.

Mavis thought the two couples must have found it easier to get along with matched pairs.

Hilary immediately saw the problem and put her fork down on her plate with a clatter.

"Well that was a surprise for you! Did you invite them to take over your room here Vilma, despite the introduction of another male into our community?"

"I did nothing definite about that, Hilary. Amanda's mother has not yet moved from Winnipeg to the hospital in London. A decision will need to be made as soon as that happens, but I can assure you these two people would fit in here beautifully. They are used to co-housing requirements and work from home, much like you do Honor. I will show you all my photos from the trip and you will see what an attractive pair they are."

"I am sure something could be arranged for them. It's a temporary situation. We could manage for three months or so."

Mavis, ever the peacemaker, was attempting to smooth the waters but she noticed Vilma still looked doubtful.

"Thank you, Mavis. The truth is I am not at all sure what the next few months will bring. The situation at Andy's farm site is not certain. There may not be a suitable place for me for some time. There are other priorities in play."

As the words left her mouth, Vilma realized she

was, for the first time, expressing doubts she had kept carefully concealed from herself.

It was a shock to everyone around the table. In Vilma's life everything seemed to progress exactly as she desired. This amount of doubt about her future was alarming to hear.

Mavis broke the silence.

"My dear, I am sure we can accommodate this lovely couple one way or another. Don't be too concerned about it for now. We are very good at problem solving as we have proved many times before.

I think you will feel different after a good night's sleep. You are probably jet lagged. I have a bottle of brandy in a cupboard here for medicinal purposes. You shall have a drop in your coffee right now and Honor can ask Faith to take the dogs out for their last run of the day."

Vilma did not argue. She was feeling very tired and disoriented. She accepted the brandy and allowed Mavis and Hilary to clear the supper dishes without objection.

A good night's sleep might bring a better attitude in the morning. Perhaps her depression was due to the huge contrast between the colourful tropics and this black and white world of Canadian winter.

~

The next morning brought news that threw Vilma's concerns into the background.

Eve was coming home earlier than expected from Santa Fe.

Hilary received the call and went immediately to see Mavis.

"It was from Eve's friend, Kylie. She said they were having a wonderful holiday in the sun and returned for a second time to the famous museum to inspect the paintings when Eve complained of feeling faint.

At first, they put it down to sunstroke, and went back to their townhouse to rest and recuperate.

The next day Eve was no better and her friend began to get alarmed. Her temperature was spiking worryingly. That's when Eve decided to return to Canada alone."

"Was she worried about paying excessive hospital rates in the States?"

"I imagine so, Mavis. In any case, we will go to London Airport and wait for her flight to arrive. As there's no telling what kind of condition she will be in, prepare for anything. If necessary we will take her straight to Emergency."

"Right. I will tell Honor what's happening while

you get out the car. I'll collect supplies from the medicine cabinet on the way."

~

There was some delay before the plane from the States arrived via Toronto Airport. Mavis and Hilary grew increasingly worried as the hours passed. The huge and crowded Toronto facility was not the most welcoming place for a person who was feeling ill. Hilary calculated the number of hours Eve had been travelling and paced around the corridors in London's more friendly airport to relieve her stress.

One thing was for sure. Whatever illness had driven Eve to leave in the midst of her holiday must, by now, be much worse.

When the passengers finally deplaned, Mavis and Hilary were gazing through the terminal windows straining for a first glance of their friend.

It was immediately obvious which passenger was Eve. She was draped in blankets, and helped down the steps from the small plane in the arms of an attendant. A wheelchair, hastily summoned from the airport was there to take her inside. Hilary and Mavis danced from foot to foot until they could get close to her. The staff person related the story.

"We were reluctant to take her on board in

Toronto as she was clearly very ill. We had a medical persona assess if she was contagious and he said she was not, but he recommended she be taken to hospital as soon as possible."

"Thank you! Thank you so much for caring for Eve. We will take over now and she will be going to Emergency right away."

Eve was not responsive when Mavis spoke to her. She managed to get a sip of water in her mouth but was reluctant to do more before the doctors saw her. Mavis sat beside Eve in the back seat of Hilary's car with the heater blowing warm air. Eve did not open her eyes all the way to London Health Sciences Centre on Commissioners Road.

By some good luck, the Emergency Department was not overwhelmed with patients and Eve was admitted after a quick assessment by a doctor. When Hilary explained that she had the same high temperature for days now, the doctor isolated her in a separate room until preliminary tests could be done. He stated that Eve's present confused and uncommunicative condition was of concern. He advised the two women to return to the waiting room as it would take some time to check everything out.

"Do you think he's afraid we have caught whatever it is Eve has?" murmured Mavis, as they paused by the metal button on the wall near the security doors that allowed exit to the outer areas.

"I can't say, Mavis. We must wait and see. I don't think we were in contact with Eve for long enough to contract anything major. Remember that a doctor in Toronto declared she was not contagious.

Just in case, they took two seats far from the nurses' booth where most of the activity was centred.

As soon as Hilary phoned home to advise Honor about their situation, she set out to find coffee and sandwiches. It looked like they were in for a long night.

Mavis thought there was nothing more disorienting than a waiting room in Emergency as the hours progressed and more patients were unloaded from ambulances and hustled straight into the Emergency area behind the huge doors.

"We were lucky to arrive before the rush, Hilary. Ambulance patients get priority.

How long do you think we will be here?"

Hilary glanced at her watch. It was well past midnight and there were no spare seats left in the waiting room. She was about to say something comforting when her name was announced. They approached the nurses' booth and were confirmed as the couple who brought in Eve Barton.

"Go on through," said the nurse as the doors opened for them. "The doctor is ready for you."

They went through to the room where they had left Eve and found her bed empty. They looked around for the doctor who had admitted Eve and found him attending to another patient. When he caught sight of them hovering nearby he led them out into the hallway and informed them that Eve had been formally admitted to the hospital for further examination.

"The high temperature is of some concern but she also has a tender area near her abdomen. It could be an infection she has contracted, but we need to investigate more closely before I can give you a definite answer. He gave them her room number and told them to call the nursing station later in the day when there would be more information about Eve's condition.

Hilary and Mavis clutched each other for support.

"At least she's safe home, and in the right place to get help," said Mavis. It was small comfort.

The cold early morning air refreshed them enough to hold back tears.

They made short work of the drive back to Harmony House with Eve's luggage, as the roads were empty of traffic.

They found Honor waiting for them with hot drinks and warm sympathy.

"You two must get some rest. I have alerted Vilma and Jannice. We will stand by for phone calls until you wake. Also, Jannice says if there is home nursing to be done for Eve, she will take a compassionate leave of absence and look after her."

They were too weary to comment. Hilary let one tear drop down her cheek and Mavis managed a weak smile before they went to their respective tower rooms and fell into bed, grateful that they were not facing this calamity alone.

Mavis's last clear thought before she drifted off to sleep was ......*this is what Harmony House is all about.*

CHAPTER 11

The atmosphere at Harmony House was dark and gloomy despite a sunny day that offered to melt the topmost layer of snow and bring warmer temperatures.

Hilary and Mavis slept well into the late morning hours and by noon they were eating porridge made by Jannice who had taken a day off and insisting she would go to the hospital with them.

"I see you two are not in the mood to eat, but the porridge will put a coating on your stomachs as my Mam always said."

The unspoken meaning was that the women would need sustenance in case of bad news ahead of them.

There was no delay. Moments after they called

the nurses' station and learned Eve could have visitors, Jannice offered to drive while Hilary and Mavis sat in the back of the small car.

Mavis wondered if there was enough room for Eve inside.

Hilary wondered if Eve was likely to be coming home with them at all. She was experiencing an unsettling premonition of bad news which she was valiantly trying to ignore.

The doctor spoke to them before they were allowed to see Eve.

"We are still doing tests but initial symptoms indicate your friend may have liver cancer."

There was a horrified silence in the room as Jannice, Mavis and Hilary absorbed this information.

"But, she was in perfect health just a few weeks ago. How could this happen?"

The doctor turned her compassionate eyes to Hilary and said liver disease has few symptoms initially.

It would not be obvious that there was anything wrong until the later stages.

Jannice recovered first.

"What stage do you think Eve has reached?"

"I do not want to speculate until we have more results. Your friend's fever has diminished and she is

RUTH HAY

quite able to tell you herself how she feels. Go in and
talk to her now. She knows what I have told you but
be hopeful. There's much that can be done."

Three women stood in the hospital hallway and
summoned their strength for Eve's sake. Inside, they
were reeling from the shock, but each of them had
dealt before with relatives suffering from serious
illness and they knew how important it was to be
optimistic.

"Right then, ladies! Let's rally around Eve and do
whatever we can."

With Jannice's admonition in mind, they wiped
away tears, and straightened shoulders, and
advanced into the private room where sun poured in
from the windows and Eve was sitting up in bed
with a smile on her face that was the best sign they
could hope for.

They sat on the bed or in the chair nearby and
asked all the questions while Eve explained what
she could.

"I was fine, honestly! Kylie and I had hours in the
museum and I adored Georgia O'Keefe's paintings.
The flowers were astonishing, of course, but there
was so much else there to wonder at. I spent the
evenings sketching and drawing ideas for my next
paintings and went to bed happy.

I was anxious to return to the museum the next

day but we had to queue to get tickets and the sun was very hot outside. When we got into the galleries the air conditioning was quite cold and I shivered for a bit. When I felt faint, I put it down to being over-excited, but later I began to feel quite unwell.

Kylie wanted to take me to a doctor in Santa Fe but I had heard horror stories about extortionate fees and I persuaded her to let me go home on my own."

"Did you have the fever then, Eve?"

"I felt ill but the fever got worse on the plane. I really can't remember much of the journey until I saw your two familiar faces at the airport. I know someone helped me at Pearson to get to the plane for London. I am just so glad to see all of you and know I am home safe again."

They occupied the remaining time with news about Vilma's trip to Jamaica and the surprise she had when she discovered Braden was a man.

Eve laughed and there was more colour in her cheeks.

Mavis thought it was a good sign of recovery when Eve asked for her sketch book and pencils to be brought on their next visit.

I can't imagine they will keep me here long, but I can make use of the remaining time. I have so many ideas in my head."

A nurse arrived to check Eve's temperature and to give her some medicine so the trio left with promises to return with art supplies and bed jackets and anything else Eve wanted.

As they walked through the hospital corridors toward the exit, Jannice remarked that she believed the nurse had administered a pain medication.

Hilary stopped and turned to her with a surprised look on her face.

"Do you think she's in pain? I couldn't see any sign of it. She looks recovered."

"She may not be telling us everything," interjected Jannice. "They would not prescribe pain pills unless there was a good reason. We don't know everything yet. Wait for more information to come."

They had to be content with Jannice's logic, but doubts lingered.

Until they had Eve safely back in Harmony House they could not be sure of her recovery. Liver cancer was a very scary diagnosis despite what they saw and heard in that hospital room.

It was three more worrying days before Eve returned to her own room at Harmony House.

She returned with a diagnosis of stage three liver

cancer and a proposed program of chemotherapy to start in the following week.

Everyone stayed positive but Eve was beginning to understand how ill she was and the knowledge frightened her. She kept the fear at bay by painting furiously on her easel by the window.

She was banned from the kitchen and Mavis took over the task of buying supplies and cooking nutritious meals for all the residents.

Vilma ordered fresh delicacies and frozen prepared meals to be delivered from the delicatessen in town. She sat with Eve whenever tea and cookies were planned, in order to interrupt her art work and make her rest. Vilma found this a good distraction from her own worries about her future and she listened while Eve described O'Keefe's Black Iris and White Bird of Paradise works.

"I will never be able to paint like that," she confessed. "But she has inspired me to be more adventurous. I would like to do some new work before......"

Vilma felt a shiver run down her back as the sentence tailed off. It was as if Eve had a presentiment about her illness and the limited time she had left. She quickly turned the discussion to the weather and the prospects of an early spring but in her heart of hearts she was afraid for Eve and decided not to repeat the incident to Mavis or Hilary.

Honor was consulting a variety of online sources about liver cancer and compiling a dossier of treatments, their premier hospital locations, and their effectiveness rates.

Jannice was making a request at work for an extended leave for compassionate reasons. She had seen patients with liver cancer before, and she wanted to be fully available if Eve needed individual care during the chemotherapy.

Life seemed to go on as usual, but beneath the surface there was concern and fear.

Hilary was the one chosen to take Eve to the cancer clinic for her first session of chemo. The atmosphere was uplifting and positive if you ignored the many headscarves and the worried partners who accompanied the patients. While Eve was being ministered to in a comfortable chair, Hilary took the chance to speak privately with the doctor assigned to her case.

"How do you account for the sudden onset of this liver problem, doctor?"

The response was honest and non-committal at the same time.

"We can't be sure. It could have been coming for a long time and only recently began to show symptoms. It could be the result of a long period of extreme stress. The body reacts differently to stress in different people."

Hilary thought back to her first view of Eve Barton and the soft hat she wore then, pulled down over her forehead to conceal the injury to her head caused by her husband's violent behaviour to her. It was difficult to reconcile the present Eve with that pitiful figure, but there was no doubt she had undergone stress for years before Mavis rescued her.

Hilary decided to ask no more questions, and she resolved to rally all the strength and faith she could in order to steer Eve through this crucial medical experience.

She knew she did not have all the knowledge that might be required, but with the expertise and goodwill residing in Harmony House, many things could be accomplished. It remained to be seen how well Eve would tolerate the sessions of chemo.

Hospital nurses and doctors had reinforced what Honor learned online. Many patients sailed through the chemo and had few distressing symptoms.

Hilary could only hope and pray that Eve was one of the lucky ones.

~

Before a month had passed, Eve was back in Harmony House. The chemotherapy had failed.

Eve was unable to tolerate the pain it caused and further investigations revealed there were other sites in her body where cancer had taken a grip.

A hospice was mentioned by the doctor in charge.

At this point, the women of Harmony House rebelled.

"She's coming home with us," demanded Mavis, through tears that roughened her voice.

"I will rent a hospital bed and anything else she needs for her comfort," insisted Vilma.

"She will be made pain free for however long she survives and we will be by her side."

Jannice spoke in the knowledge that she was competent to co-ordinate medical services, and to administer a morphine pump under the supervision of a visiting nurse. She had already received permission to take a leave of absence from her current home care position.

Hilary was immensely grateful that Jannice had

the expertise that would allow Eve to have this option.

Everyone would rally round to make Eve's last days as comfortable and pleasant as possible.

Hilary was relieved to have this united support and, once again, she blessed the day she and Mavis had concocted the scheme to find a home for themselves and other compatible women. She could only marvel at how well they had selected these women. At times of stress, they always drew together in mutual compassion. She wondered how many families had the benefit of such support and doubted whether any families in today's world could find members who could devote time and energy so willingly. Jannice's home care job demonstrated how few family members were free to dedicate themselves to their elders. Many had families of their own and jobs that were necessary to maintain a roof over their heads. Other families were spread out over the earth these days and could not give the twenty-four hour care that was sometimes required.

Hilary decided she would take on the role of ensuring every person at Harmony House who is involved in Eve's care, would, in turn, be cared for by her. She would monitor schedules and ensure regular breaks. If the weather improved, she would insist on Eve getting outside for even a few minutes to breathe the air and see the beginning of spring arrive in Mavis's garden.

She was not good at bedside stuff, herself, but she would ensure the others lacked for nothing.

If music should be needed to lift spirits, she would supply it from Mavis's collection.

If special foods were required, she would obtain them, online if necessary.

She would enlist Honor's help to keep ahead of laundry. Eve's room should always be bright and fresh with the flowers she loved.

If Eve expressed the desire to see friends or acquaintances from her earlier life, Hilary would find them and convey them to her bedside.

She would do all that any person could do to make this transition from life to death as easy as possible.

CHAPTER 12

Everything else was set aside while Eve was spending her last days in Harmony House.

Vilma encouraged Andy to stay at the farm and get on with the building work. She did not want his presence to disturb the established routines around Eve that were keeping all in the house on an even keel.

There was an atmosphere of solemn peace interspersed with laughter and fun when Jannice entertained Eve with her family tales or Mavis loaned Marble to sit comfortable by Eve's side purring in contentment.

Faith helped by becoming an expert dishwasher loader.

Honor had serious discussions with Eve

regarding her final wishes. She was the only one given this information.

"I do not want to spoil the lovely work these women are doing to keep me cheerful, Honor.

Please do not share what I have said to you with them, until you must. Thank you for your help."

Honor was almost overcome by being the recipient of Eve's trust and gladly took on the task to relieve Eve's mind.

"Anything you need, call on me at any time, Eve."

On good days, Eve sat by the window for an hour and painted. At these times, she was imbued with an air of sheer delight in creating something that would survive her.

Once or twice she requested a Sunday gathering at her bedside where she asked for the monthly house meeting to continue while a picnic meal was served on trays. She listened to the concerns of the house members and gave useful advice. In this way she maintained her role in the co-housing project and reminded them she was still alive and able to contribute.

～

March passed, and a brighter April began to signal winter was finally relinquishing its grasp on the countryside.

Vilma drove with the dogs to Andy's farm to see the building progress. He had told her the insurance claim was finally paid, but he did not say how much money was available.

She approached the lane to the barn with some trepidation. Astrid and Oscar were straining against their harnesses in the rear seats of the car. Their reactions were obviously based on their delight at a reunion with Andy after a long spell of missing him.

She saw the new white fencing and the drystone wall constructed from the stones of the old farmhouse foundations.

She saw the two-storey addition to the barn forming an L shape and marvelled at how much had been accomplished with the volunteer help of Andy's old team.

He was waiting for her before she cut the engine of the car. He opened up the rear door first and released the dogs who promptly engulfed him in a flurry of paws and licks and frantic circling suggesting they were saying in doggy language, 'Come on! Let's go!'

He took them into the barn and closed the door before turning to greet Vilma.

She was waiting by the car and wondering how to negotiate the ground that was a builder's mess of mud, debris and frozen sections.

Andy solved her problem by lifting her up into his arms and walking carefully from stone slabs to drier patches until they were inside the new extension.

'My darling Vilma! It's been too long but I know how hard things have been for all of you at Harmony House. It's so good to see you again."

She was instantly enveloped in a huge hug that gave weight to his words, but she discovered there was a space inside her that was preventing her from answering him with a whole heart. It might have been the need to preserve her emotions lest Eve saw what the daily tasks of caring for her were costing. It might have been the shock of seeing how far things had progressed here at the farm in her absence. Whatever the source, she felt unable to be wholehearted with him.

"You have been busy, Andy! I can't believe how much you have done. Is this a double storey kennels structure? That's unusual."

Andy put aside a tiny dash of disappointment at her first reaction to him, and focussed on his pride at what had been accomplished so far.

"It was Dave's idea to capitalize on the ground

available to us. The upper level is designed for work spaces mostly. Come on up and see!"

"He bounded up what Vilma saw as a flimsy ladder and turned to give her a hand with the last part.

In front of her stretched an area of fifty feet or so with a sloping attic roof. It was divided by partitions into three rooms, each with two windows. On one side, the view was of the road to the barn and on the other there was a long gentle slope from the ridge to the familiar stream bordered by willows and beyond to more farmland.

She saw something of a business office set-up in one of the sections in the loft and in the second there was a camp bed, a hot plate, a four-shelf storage unit and a sink, already plumbed in. A shiny new stove, still encased in plastic, stood waiting for electrical connections. An old easy chair that was one of the few items saved from the drowned wreck of Andy's farmhouse, sagged in the corner by the rear window.

She stepped over to this window and gazed at the view while attempting to control her emotions.

Andy had moved on. He was living here. She could see no attempt to build the dream house for the two of them. This was a bachelor's pad, a rough and ready spot for a busy, working man.

Behind her, Andy continued speaking about his business.

"I have several clients already. Mostly puppy training so far, but I am looking out for any dog with potential to be a competition animal. The lower level with temporary dog housing is almost completed. We gave priority to that. The bookings will come along later in the season when people want to travel south.

Oh, and Vilma, I would like to borrow Astrid and Oscar for demonstrations to show what dogs can achieve in agility and obedience. *And....*" His voice rose in excitement. "I found a farmer not too far away with a small flock of sheep who is willing to let me use them to see what your Australian dogs' instincts in herding can do. A movie of that would be a great advert for us. That won't happen until later this month when the sheep come out with their lambs from the winter quarters.

Isn't that ace! Astrid and Oscar will love the exercise. They are looking a bit out of shape. *Not your fault*, of course, Vilma! It's been a tough winter for all you women."

He stopped at last. She had neither turned around to face him nor responded to his enthusiasm.

A jolt of fear struck him in the gut. What was

going on? This was definitely not the reaction he had expected.

Vilma waited to gather herself together. Andy had unconsciously revealed so much by his words. It was necessary now for her to confirm what she suspected.

She turned, and to him her face was like an unreadable mask.

"Is this what you chose to do with the insurance money, Andy? I imagine it was it not as much as you had hoped to get."

"Correct! The old farmhouse was not worth much in the end and the barn survived well. I decided to maximize the potential and go ahead with the build here while I had the expertise of the guys to help me. They've been amazing! Turning up here in all weathers for nothing more than a pot of chilli and a beer. It was much like the old days at the station. I couldn't have done all this without them, Vilma."

"Yes, I can see that, Andy. You have done a great deal and your business is off to a good start. I am very glad for you."

In spite of her approving words, he knew there was still something lacking. Where was the Vilma who had encouraged his efforts to renew his life? Where were her smiles and her welcoming arms?

He stepped toward her and reached out to enfold her. She sank into his embrace but it still felt as if she was holding something back.

What Vilma Smith was fighting so hard, was her desire to weep in his arms, to ask for comfort, to make the present disappear and bring the past to life again. That past time when they were together for every decision and every idea to promote their future.

In her heart of hearts, she had to acknowledge the hard truth.

Andy had moved on.

He no longer needed her.

She would never be happy living in this extended barn loft.

There would never be a real need for him to invest in a separate house for them.

He was content with what he had here, and it was not a lifestyle in which she could fully participate.

The sad truths sank down into her soul but she did not have the heart to tell him what she now knew.

Far more kind, to let him discover all this for himself as he undoubtedly would, in time.

For now, she would ask for nothing from him. She would not lie to him but she would be true to herself and leave soon to lick her wounds.

Life without Andy Patterson loomed ahead, but not quite yet. She had not yet decided which was the better route for him. Slow realization of their differences, or a quick cut and gone.

It was a saddened Vilma Smith who left the big red Patterson barn behind as it disappeared from her rear view mirror.

The dogs were happy with their day.

The chilling April winds that made their appearance as she bid farewell to Andy, had entered into her heart.

She decided to leave the next step up to Andy. At Harmony House there were more important matters to deal with.

CHAPTER 13

Honor stopped Hilary on her way into the house after her morning in town with her 'oldies'.

"Hilary, could I have a word with you? I have coffee on the go. That wind is still like ice."

The two women went downstairs from the porch to Honor's work and living space. Hilary gladly accepted the proffered coffee and wrapped her chilled fingers around the mug.

"What can I do for you, Honor?"

"It's not for me, really. I just feel I need to let you know that Eve has entrusted me with her will and her final wishes."

"Oh! When was this?"

"It was some weeks ago now. I believe it indicates

how well she is prepared for her final days and I hope you are not upset because she chose me. Eve said she knew how much you were dealing with and she wanted to save you the trouble.

She has nothing much to leave, Hilary, so I think a solicitor was not necessary. There is one thing she did want and that is something I will need help with."

"What is that?"

"Eve expressed a wish to see her husband, Howard Dobrinski, one last time."

"Surely not! He almost killed her…… *and* Mavis! Why on earth would she want to see that awful man again?"

As the words left her lips, Hilary realized how inappropriate it was to question the last wish of a dying woman.

"I am sorry, Honor. I am just blown away by this request. My feelings are, clearly, *not* the important consideration in this matter. How will we accomplish this for Eve?"

"Well, I have made enquiries. Howard Dobrinski is no longer in prison. He completed his sentence for aggravated assault rather earlier than expected. Apparently, by all accounts, he was a model prisoner.

He remains on probation and is forbidden to approach his ex-wife but I can't track down his current location. Do you think, Mavis, with her courthouse connections could help?"

"I will ask her. Are you sure this is what Eve wants?"

"I had my doubts, Hilary, but she must want to make peace with him for her own reasons."

In the silence while both wondered what those reasons might be, came Honor's last and most difficult question.

"How long do you think Eve has?"

Hilary pursed her lips. It was a question on the minds of all the residents of Harmony House.

"I couldn't say for sure, but it's probably better to try to find this man as soon as possible while Eve can still communicate her wishes to him."

Hilary went upstairs to see who was on duty with Eve and found Mavis seated by her bed, knitting. She looked up when Hilary entered and came over to the door to see what she needed.

"Can Eve be left for a few minutes? I have to talk to you."

"She's resting now. Jannice checked her morphine a half-hour ago. We'll leave the door partially open in case she calls out."

Mavis expressed similar shock as did Hilary when she heard about Eve's request, but her mind quickly turned toward who she would consult about finding Howard Dobrinski's current location.

"There will be a record of his residence since he is on probation. As I was involved in his trial evidence, I should be permitted to have the information you need.

Leave it with me, Hilary. You go to Eve's bedside while I make a few calls and we'll see what happens.

Mavis returned to relieve Hilary after only fifteen minutes.

Once more they stepped outside, leaving the door open behind them.

"Did you learn anything useful?"

"I did better than that! I found him and I talked to him."

"Really! That was fast. How did he sound?"

"He sounded like a completely improved individual! He cried when I told him about Eve's condition."

"No!"

"Not only that, but before I could make a request, he asked if he could possibly come to see her and begged me to bring him to wherever he could speak to her."

"Mavis! Tell me you did not reveal our address to him."

"Of course, not! I don't want that man turning up here in the night as he did at Camden Corners.

Neither do I want to spend any time in a car with him."

"I understand perfectly, Mavis. We'll employ a cab driver to pick him up and take him home again and we'll restrict his time with Eve in case he upsets her in any way. Someone must be in the room with them. I suggest Vilma, since she has not had any prior nasty encounters with him."

"Good suggestion! Vilma will not tolerate any nonsense from him.

"But first, I must contact his probation officer to request permission for the visit."

"Of course, you must. It will give us some short time to get prepared.

When all was managed to their satisfaction, the women held a last meeting to ensure everything possible would go well for Eve's visit with her ex-husband.

Mavis spoke first.

"What we want is a quick in and out and no bad effects. I will stand by the door when he arrives. He heard my evidence in court and he knows I will not hesitate to send him back to prison if he puts one foot wrong."

All that remained was to set a date for the meeting.

Jannice was consulted.

"She will be clearer first thing in the day, but she won't have much energy, particularly if it is an emotional confrontation."

"Honor got the impression it was to be about reconciliation rather than an angry shouting match."

"In that case, Hilary, I think you should plan for this to happen in a day or two at most."

Jannice's words sent a chill through Hilary. She asked Mavis to make the arrangements and asked Jannice to inform Eve.

"If Eve reacts badly to the idea, we will cancel the whole thing. Agreed?"

"Of course."

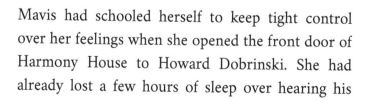

Mavis had schooled herself to keep tight control over her feelings when she opened the front door of Harmony House to Howard Dobrinski. She had already lost a few hours of sleep over hearing his voice on the phone and she was not willing to give him any more power over her wellbeing.

She handed him over to Vilma, as soon as his coat and hat were stowed in the closet, and retreated to her tower room to wait. Her hands were shaking from just that quick look at him.

Vilma was surprised to see Eve's husband. He looked much like any other man you would pass on the street without noticing. He had dark hair, combed carefully after a recent haircut. His suit and coat were worn but clean, and he had held a cap in his workman's hands which he turned round and round, displaying his nervousness.

Vilma led the way upstairs without saying anything.

Jannice met him outside Eve's door and cautioned him about his demeanour, and also, to be prepared for the shock of his ex-wife's appearance. Vilma then went inside first, and talked briefly to Eve.

When Eve was ready, she returned to invite Howard in. She told him she would be waiting inside the washroom in case she was needed.

He nodded in acceptance of these precautions. It was clear to him that these women were acting together in Eve's best interests and they would tolerate nothing that might disturb their friend.

Vilma heard very little of the conversation by the bedside. Voices were low and slow and there were a number of pauses. She thought there might be a soft sobbing sound at one point but chose not to interrupt.

A moment later, there was a tap on the washroom door and she found Dobrinski on the other side. One quick glance showed her Eve was still sitting comfortably, propped up against her pillows with her eyes closed. She took the man's arm and escorted him out and downstairs to the front door. As he fastened up his coat again, he took a deep breath and asked her to thank all the women for looking after Eve so well.

"She always had a great fear of hospitals, you know? Something to do with an accident when she was a young child. What you are doing here for Eve is wonderful. I cannot thank you enough."

His voice choked up with tears and Vilma watched him walk swiftly down the front path to where the cab was waiting for him.

The household, with the exception of Faith, gathered in the kitchen for a coffee and pastry to debrief after this troubling experience. The general consensus was, that it had gone well due to their good planning.

Jannice, who was the last to arrive, reported that

Eve seemed at peace now although she was very tired.

Since they were all together, Mavis took the opportunity to ask the question that was on everyone's mind.

"How long does Eve have?"

"Not long now. If there is anything you need to say to her, I would not wait. She will soon drift off and be mostly unresponsive."

There was a collective gasp around the table and with a single impulse in mind, the women reached for the nearest hand and grasped it tightly.

Honor was the first to recover. She cleared her throat to get everyone's attention.

"In that case, I will follow Eve's orders, and read to you all, her final wishes, before it is too late."

Only Hilary was prepared for this announcement. She nodded to Honor to fetch the document and when she had left to get the elevator, Hilary proceeded to pour fresh coffee and fill in the details Honor had told her previously.

Honor held herself in control on the short return elevator ride and did as Eve had requested in a simple and sympathetic way.

My Dear Friends,

Do not weep for me now. I have had the finest care and help from all of you, and my years at Harmony

House have been full of rich and happy times. You gave me safety and a new life.

My wishes are few.

Inform Kylie when I am gone. She will tell my friends at the Art Club.

Please, no announcements in the newspaper.

No funeral. Just a quick, private cremation. Scatter my ashes in Mavis's garden that I have enjoyed so much.

I do have a few bequests.

To Hilary, I leave the remaining money from my inheritance, so that she can offset the expenses incurred by her generosity to me and to Faith.

To Mavis, I leave all my art and possessions with the exception of the three paintings she will find dedicated to Vilma for her new life with Andy.

To Jannice, who has been a rock and comfort to me these last months, I leave my online art clothing business, Eve's Garden, with all the unsold stock, to do with as she wishes.

To Honor I give any and all future proceeds from the sale of my stored paintings, now in the Byron Library, to be shared with Faith in any way she sees fit.

My last request is that my room in Harmony House be used to give shelter to any compatible woman or man who needs a temporary home and who can afford the monthly fee. I am thinking of the two cousins from Manitoba, of course, but that decision is not mine to make.

I wish you all health and happiness as you move forward.

Think of me in the sunshine, painting happily or cooking something delicious in the kitchen.

I am sorry to leave you all so soon but so blessed to have known you.

With Love,

Eve Barton.

When Honor finished reading the letter, there was not one dry eye around the table.

She filled in the emotional pause by adding the information that Eve had set in place all the legal and financial requirements for her bequests, including those for the cremation.

"How do we proceed now, given this information about Eve's generous last wishes?"

Mavis passed around a box of tissues. Eyes and cheeks were wiped dry and noses blown, while this new idea was processed.

As no else responded to her question, Hilary took the lead.

"My feeling is that I want to thank Eve in person, while I can. It is so brave of her to think of all of us at a time like this. Her letter is incredibly moving and demands an action from me. That does not mean everyone should feel the same way. Please, each woman here should do as she feels best. These are unusual circumstances."

Jannice then repeated her advice about timing.

"Wait until tomorrow morning. Go in separately and do not stay long. Even if Eve's eyes are closed, she will hear you. Hold her hand while you speak and be as uplifting as you can manage, ladies.

God bless us all!"

~

Almost as if it were meticulously planned, the women chose their individual moment to speak their last words to Eve.

Hilary was first and earliest. Jannice was still at Eve's bedside checking her pulse and adjusting her medication. She moved into the washroom to clean Eve's glass and washcloths and by the time she emerged, Hilary had gone.

Vilma was next. While she was out with the dogs, she had decided to thank Eve without mentioning the fact that her gift of paintings was not likely to be displayed in a new house shared by Andy. This in no way detracted from Eve's kindness. Vilma would always treasure her thoughtfulness.

Honor chose not to speak to Eve. After the

experience of reading the letter to the household, she felt she would not be able to stay calm in Eve's presence. Painful thoughts of missing her sister's death were plaguing her, and she was sure she would overreact and do more harm than good.

Later the same day, as the sun rose in an April sky, Mavis looked out of her window and gasped. The daffodils that had been reluctant to open in the recent cold snap were now blooming all over the garden. It was a field of pale gold stretching to the woods.

She ran downstairs to the garage and retrieved her garden shears and a large crystal vase from storage. Then she went back to the front entrance and soon knocked on Faith's door. The girl was sleeping late as it was a Saturday, but her sleepy voice responded.

Mavis went in and explained what she wanted Faith to do. That got her out of bed quickly and into her jacket and pants, pulled over pyjamas.

The task was to fill the vase with daffodils for Eve's room. They picked the best of the blooms and Mavis took the chance to explain to Faith everything that had happened in the last few days.

"Aunt Honor has seemed very sad about Eve, and

I did not want to ask too many questions, Mavis. Thanks for telling me. Eve was always very kind to me. She often made me snacks at odd times, and fed me when I was studying late at night. Would it be all right if I come with you to see her one last time?"

"Of course it would, Faith. I am glad you asked."

They went to Eve's room with hands full of flowers. Faith had found a second container lurking under the garden bench and filled it as well.

They found Eve sitting up in bed and quite conscious. Her eyes glittered with delight when she saw the daffodils and her breathing deepened to catch the scent of fresh-cut stems and the glorious bright yellow flowers. Mavis set the crystal vase on Eve' bedside table while Faith took the other to the window where it sat in the sunlight and spread the true scent of spring throughout the room.

Suddenly it was not a scene of death and dying but a place of ever-renewed hope.

Faith stayed by the window while Eve and Mavis spoke privately for a moment. There was no crying. Just smiles and hands clasped together.

Faith thought of her mother's last days in the stark hospital room and knew this peaceful place was far better than that sterile environment where no one thought to explain to a frightened girl what would happen to her once her mother was gone. She could now see that dreadful experience as the beginning of her deep antagonism to authority figures; an antagonism that led her into so much trouble.

As each year of what she mentally termed, 'her rescue', progressed, she knew she owed a debt to every woman in Harmony House; a debt she might never be able to repay in full.

As if Eve had read her thoughts, she signalled to Faith to come closer.

Her voice was weak. Faith leaned in to hear her words and Mavis gave up her seat after one last, soft kiss on Eve's forehead.

"My dear girl, you have been such a breath of fresh air in this house, much like these glorious daffodils!

I want to tell you to keep growing and caring for others. You are capable of doing much good in the world. You are unique.

Thank your aunt for me. Now off you go and enjoy the day."

Eve sank back. The brief conversation had taken the last of her strength but it was something Faith would remember for the rest of her life.

Mavis and Faith hugged once they were on the balcony landing again. Jannice was waiting with the hospice nurse.

"How is she?"

"She is happy and content."

"Good," said Jannice, and the two carers went into the room together.

CHAPTER 14

The death of someone close can have different effects on those who are left behind.

At Harmony House these effects varied from sheer relief that Eve's pain was over, to a feeling of regret for words left unsaid.

As the days passed and Eve's final wishes were fulfilled to the last detail, the atmosphere in the house lightened. April was morphing into May with warm breezes and sunshine that surprised everyone with its intensity.

Life began to resume its usual routines, but not without significant changes.

Mavis spent every available daylight hour in her garden, when she was not helping Louise Ridley.

Vilma received a text from Amanda informing

her that her mother was scheduled to fly with her to London, Ontario to begin her cancer treatment. Vilma's plans would need to be speeded up to accommodate this.

Jannice made arrangements to accompany Mitchell on his delayed trip to Toronto to investigate the original locations of the Grace Marks' drama.

Honor made the decision to spend time in Kingston in July, with the Jeffries family, to give Faith a break away from her growing school responsibilities.

Hilary was stunned to discover how long she had spent, isolated in the house while Eve was requiring support. Her first drive to Byron revealed changes happening nearby. A new housing development had grown up on the other side of Oxford Street, called West 5. This, according to the billboards, was a Sifton building project, incorporating solar technology for Millennials who wished energy saving residences.

Not only was the traffic in the area increasing, but as Hilary passed the intersection with Westdel Bourne, she saw large earthmoving vehicles re-grading the area for a future light commercial plaza to include a Tim Hortons.

On her return from shopping in Byron, she hastened to inform Mavis of these incursions.

"Well, it seems the city is beginning to encroach on our secluded and private crescent!"

"I am sure it will be many years before development reaches this quiet side road. It will mean better bus services and more amenities, Hilary, and as we grow older that is a benefit."

Hilary was not convinced. She was not pleased with the pace of change. She would prefer to have inconveniences rather than be surrounded by vast housing estates and their accompanying problems.

She decided to pay more attention to announcements in the newspaper regarding such developments and to attend City Hall forums whenever public input was requested.

This matter was tabled at the next Sunday dinner and discussion, but it was soon passed over in favour of other more immediate concerns. Vilma needed a decision about accommodating Amanda and Braden. Jannice's imminent departure for Toronto brought up the matter of housekeeping and cooking duties.

Hilary agreed to monitor the stocking of kitchen supplies. Honor promised to keep an eye on the common areas and vacuum and dust as required in Jannice's absence.

No one could replace Eve, their Kitchen Queen. Mavis attempted to fill in the gap by offering to cook meals but she was quickly shouted down.

"Mavis! You have enough on your plate with the garden and Louise's foster children arriving very soon.

Your contribution to cooking will be fresh herbs and vegetables from the garden. The rest of us will do what we can. I suggest using the whiteboard to inform us if a large dish is planned for sharing."

Vilma, who felt guilty about her lack of culinary skills, promptly added her intention to provide a substantial dish from her favourite catering company for their twice-monthly Sunday dinners."

"That's very generous of you, Vilma. Perhaps someone will take a cooking course and help us out, but I do not believe we are in any danger of starving, not with a Tim Hortons soon to arrive close by!"

Hilary's comment made the others laugh but it was laughter tinged with regret. No one could be the cook that Eve was. It was not only her food they would miss; it was also her warm and welcoming presence.

Hilary vetoed the prior plan to use Mavis's tower room for the cousins.

"It's no longer necessary to dislodge Mavis. Eve

wished us to offer them her room on a temporary basis."

"If we do that, there is a problem with beds. They will need two beds. I am glad to refresh the room for them and do anything that is required, including purchasing two single beds. They will be right beside the kitchen and the elevator, which is convenient. Braden will rent a car. I know they are anxious not to disrupt our routines and one or both of them will be at the hospital most of the time."

"That sound good, Vilma. Do you still feel confident that they will fit in here with us?"

Mavis was expressing the doubts of all of them. It seemed too soon to be replacing their Eve.

"I can only speak from my observations of a week's holiday with the pair, but I know they are good people, younger of course, and with busy online lives. They are very grateful for the opportunity to share Harmony House."

Honor was acutely conscious of the privileges all these women had bestowed on her. She suddenly saw an opportunity to repay some of that generosity.

"I am more than willing to share my work space with Amanda and Braden. They will love being close to the garden and I have good tech connections they can use. That will make up for only having one bedroom."

Honor's helpful idea was applauded by all, and the matter was shelved for now.

Time would tell what the effect on Harmony House would be of a man around the place on a daily basis.

Braden's presence would be more consistent than Andy's had been. Vilma wondered how long it would be before anyone noticed the latter's absence.

Hilary wondered if Braden could cook.

Mavis hoped Mandy's mother would respond well to her treatment. It was much too soon to have bereaved people in their environment again.

Honor was looking forward to having talks with other young people who worked on the cutting edge of business technology.

Jannice was delighted to be going to Toronto to meet Mitchell, leaving far behind the memories of Eve's last hours. When she returned to Harmony House again, Eve's room would look different and it would belong to two different people. Eve's spirit would be gone.

Vilma felt enthused by the prospect of redecorating Eve's room. Most of the furnishings were older items from Hilary's Camden Corners house and could do with being replaced.

She realized this activity was a way of compensating for the loss of her plan to decorate a home for Andy and herself. She would enter into this decorating task with a whole heart and do her best.

~

Once more Harmony House was a hive of activity.

Vilma chose paint colours to harmonize with Eve's paintings and refreshed her old room with new details, including fresh towels and accessories in the washroom. The set of new twin beds was installed with matching nightstands, bedding and comforters. She looked for decorative items that were more neutral so that Braden would not feel surrounded by a purely feminine vibe. Anything small and personal to Eve, was removed and saved, to be offered later as souvenirs to the women of the house. Vilma secured her three paintings and stored them carefully. For now, she did not want to see them hung. The reminder of their intended location with Andy was still too raw.

She took the dogs to the barn a few times for sessions with Andy but she did not enter the extension.

Once they ventured to the farm where the flock of sheep were now outdoors for the summer and, for a while, it felt like old times as she watched Andy expertly handle her dogs' behaviour and restrain their impulse to dive into the flock and scatter them everywhere.

One of Andy's pals accompanied them in order to make an advertising video so Vilma was relieved of the worry about a personal conversation with Andy. She had no good news to give him.

She knew he had promised to resume weekly lawn maintenance at Harmony House. Away from the barn, and all the memories related to the farm, she hoped she could deal with him without too much emotion getting in the way.

Amanda arrived at Harmony House with Vilma after the two of them took Maureen to London Health Sciences Centre and saw her settled there.

Mandy, as she preferred to be called, was enthralled by her new accommodations and was so pleasant and grateful to everyone that she was an immediate success. When she discovered there was a gap in meal preparations, she gladly volunteered to treat the women to exotic dishes of South America that were a delight for all of them. Mandy insisted they had the best-equipped kitchen she had ever seen and set to work there with enthusiasm. When her mother's treatment schedule was in place, the timing would change, but she was determined to pull her weight in the food department.

After two weeks, Braden arrived with the bulk of their luggage and a routine emerged which included work sessions shared with Honor, visits to the hospital and walks in the woods or nearby parks with Vilma or Faith and the dogs. They also spent time exploring the city and Braden stated London was a charming place with many amenities and a thriving business sector.

Hilary put the cousins in touch with her son, Desmond, who also reported they were knowledgeable entrepreneurs who could be a good resource to others in London.

Jannice had left for Toronto to tour sites related to Irish maidservant, Grace Marks. While in their hotel, they discussed Mitchell's outline for a book featuring other true Irish tales and history. Jannice insisted he must return to the London area with her to see the village of Lucan, and hear about the infamous clan of Black Donnellys who once lived there.

For all the Harmony House residents, life resumed a forward pace almost as if the sudden death of Eve had reminded them to use their time as productively as possible.

CHAPTER 15

Mavis planted and pruned furiously for a few weeks then turned her attention to Louise Ridley.

Dennis and Louise were now working together, to make the dream of a new family come true.

Dr. Liston had been consulting with Louise all winter and was happy to declare her former patient restored to good mental health.

At their final meeting, Dr. Liston was very positive in her comments.

"I am here for you, Louise, whenever you feel uncertain or confused but I can confidently say you are ready for the new responsibilities you wish to undertake. Remember that you will be dealing with children who have been through trauma. Your own recent experiences will give you special insight into what the children are going through. I know you will do your best for them and make a difference in their lives."

Louise felt encouraged by her psychologist's assessment. She knew she was ready. The courses she had taken, together with spells at Merrymount Children's Home, had prepared her for a variety of situations but, nonetheless, she was relieved to know that, in addition to her husband's full support, she could still count on Mavis Montgomery.

There was another more surprising person in her corner. Faith Jeffries had expressed interest in helping to orient the foster children.

"Look, Mrs. Ridley, I have been through the foster mill and I know what it is like for kids who are trying to keep their heads above water. Mavis may have mentioned I am thinking of specializing in social work with children and young adults. I would like the chance to work with you and your husband, if you think I can be of any help?"

Louise was overjoyed to accept this offer. The one thing that still bothered her about fostering was the lack of experience in her background. As an only child, she had once had a small group of carefully-selected children with whom she was allowed to play. That was many years ago and she felt out of touch with today's youngsters. Faith would definitely fill that gap for her and for Dennis.

Although her Social Services' supervisor had assured her she possessed the prime attributes of compassion and caring, she badly wanted to succeed with this most important project and she decided she would leave no resource untapped.

~

When the phone summons arrived for Louise to come to the offices downtown, she was thrilled and scared in equal measure.

She breathed deeply for a minute then phoned Mavis first.

Mavis expressed her delight to Louise. She did not, however, reveal that she had already been contacted by a former colleague, who knew her connection to Louise and Dennis Ridley.

"Mavis, give me your honest opinion. Do you think your neighbour can tackle a difficult case? I know it's too soon, but we are desperate here. There are three youngsters involved. It's a horrendous situation that was high profile in the local news when the case first came to the attention of the courts. The parents will be in prison for several years, most likely. The entire story is sad beyond belief and there will be a possible future separation since one of the girls may go to live with her biological father."

Mavis easily recalled the case as it had occupied several columns in the local newspaper. She knew it would be a challenge for Louise and Dennis but she also knew the depth of love in Louise's heart.

A heart that had been broken and mended again knew all about pain, and loss, and recovery.

"Shannon, I thank you for contacting me about this. I know social services will be watching and helping. We both know there were mistakes made in the original case and the foster situation must repair some of that damage. I can assure you of my help. I live right next door to the Ridleys. I believe Louise Ridley will be exactly what these children need at the present moment. Beyond that, neither of us can see."

Mavis accompanied Louise downtown where they sat in an office and listened to the official version of the events leading up to the death of the youngest child in the family.

The physical and psychological profiles of the remaining three siblings were produced, with recommendations as to schooling for the older girl and preschool attendance for the middle child, a boy.

"Of course, future plans may be put aside for now. What is vital is that these children feel safe and cared for in the short term. You can expect broken nights and tantrums. Consistent rules and careful listening are crucial, as you will soon realize.

It is our policy to leave you unmonitored for the first week but you must contact us immediately if any situation arises in which you feel yourself to be inadequate."

Louise listened to this fairly-impersonal description of the children's former lives and her heart quailed inside her. The pressure of Mavis's hand on her arm kept her from blurting out something to the effect that the children had not yet been named to her as individuals. They were still case numbers; objects to be dealt with.

She was handed a sheaf of paperwork and soon left the office to be conducted to a playroom where several children were occupied with games and dress-up clothes in a mock theatre set up.

Louise could not identify the children for whom she was about to be responsible until Mavis found the relevant page of the paperwork and pointed out the name tags.

Shania was one of the older children in the playroom. At twelve years of age she was tall and thin, with a head of thick brown curls cascading down her back. Her brother Tyrone was four. He was building a tower of blocks with his big sister watching his every move. He had darker skin and black hair and was competing for blocks with his baby sister, named Betsy, who looked very much like him, with a similar 'bowl-cut' hairstyle.

Anyone watching the scene would know these three belonged together. Louise's heart went out to them immediately.

"What do we do now?" she whispered to Mavis.

"Just watch for a few minutes. See how they interact. Shania is looking over here already. If she approaches, tell her the truth, otherwise smile in a friendly manner if she catches your eye."

Many things were racing through Louise's head as she followed Mavis's instructions but she refused to be intimidated by the task ahead of her. She focussed on the way Shania protected the little ones. When Tyrone grabbed a block from Betsy's hand, she quickly found another similar block and offered it to her sister before she could break into tears.

Shania will be a real asset to me and to the children. She is a born carer. I must try to get her on my side without seeming to replace her influence with her little family.

Mavis was assembling in her head all the information she had gathered from sources, formal and informal. This was going to be a challenge, all right. The older girl would be in school and the two younger ones would behave much like babies, regressing into earlier stages of their development.

Two babies at once!

She was sure Louise and Dennis had been chosen because they had more than enough space, no other children to care for, and the time to devote to these three.

She ran over in her mind the preparations Louise had made. The nursery was very well equipped. The toy baskets were full of all kinds of educational toys recommended by experts. There were four available bedrooms on one floor close to the master bedroom. Shania could have her choice of bedroom styles. There was a family room or playroom with television and a kitchen table big enough for five or six. She made note of the need to purchase a second high chair.

Beyond all these material elements, was the overriding knowledge that what these children needed most was not things. They needed love and protection, and understanding.

One look at Louise Ridley's face told her she need not worry on that score.

~

Mavis's car was stuffed full. When she drove into the Ridley's driveway she was pleased to see that Dennis had received her messages and reached home in time to greet his new family.

She had cautioned Dennis to stay in the background at first. The children had enough to adjust to and their experiences with men had not been positive of late. He helped Louise out of the car and then stayed back to unload the small amount of luggage that came with the children. The two younger ones were already gripping their favourite soft toys as if they were a lifeline.

Dennis knew Louise was nervous. He intended to support her in every way possible but he was reassured by the presence of Mavis. This was a new venture for him also. He had seen how Louise recovered from her mental issues and became, once again, the woman he first married. He was keenly aware of the role he played in her breakdown and was determined to make up for his past neglect.

At work, he made it clear he would require time off for family matters, sometimes at a moment's notice. He did not reveal the reasons for this unusual request but his superiors valued his contributions sufficiently that they did not immediately ask for further information.

While Mavis and Louise took the younger pair to

the main floor playroom and washroom, Dennis introduced himself to the older girl and asked if she would like to choose her own bedroom upstairs.

She waited to see where her siblings were being taken, and by whom, then followed Dennis making sure she kept well away from close contact with him.

Shania was distracted by the beautiful rooms she was shown. Each was nicer than the one before. She loved the lilac room the best but did not say so until she ascertained where her brother and sister would sleep. Louise and Dennis had decided to place Betsy in the small nursery, once an extra clothes storage room, close to their master suite. It had an adjoining door to a second room. This was where Tyrone would sleep. Louise intended to leave the door open in case one or the other woke up and needed comfort in the night.

The lilac room with a side window looking out on the property next door was recently re-decorated and included a desk with chair and computer, as well as pretty drapes matching the bedding. The built-in closet was huge, far bigger than anything Shania had ever known and inside it were several hangers holding outfits she thought must be there by mistake, as they were clearly new.

Dennis stood by the open door and watched her explore, but when she spent minutes making sure

RUTH HAY

the closet doors opened and shut easily and had no locks, he began to wonder if the girl had once been imprisoned in a similar small space as a punishment.

This one realization did more to prepare him for foster fatherhood than anything written on a psychological profile ever could. He burned with anger that a child could be mistreated in such a way and also cautioned himself to be prepared for further revelations. He made a mental note to install a sliding lock on the inside of Shania's bedroom door once she was settled in.

Leaving Shania to make herself at home, he returned to the playroom and found Louise comforting a sobbing Betsy while Mavis rocked Tyrone in her arms.

What had gone wrong so soon?

"What can I do to help?"

Mavis turned to him and calmly asked him to bring the tray of milk and cookies from the kitchen countertop.

Louise had bought sippy cups with funny animal antics on the outside that appeared only when the liquid inside was consumed. He carried the tray carefully to the playroom and placed it on a low table near his wife. Mavis, with Tyrone in her arms, and using a happy, light tone of voice he had never heard from her before, explained in a sing-song way that the little girl was calling for her mama. Obviously, she had expected to be taken to her mother and not to this strange house with people she did not know.

"It's part of the adjustment period, Dennis. You can expect much more of this. Don't give them any false information and break their trust. Try to distract them. I think Shania will be the one to interpret matters in a way they will eventually understand."

He thought back to the girl testing the closet doors and a shiver ran over him as he imagined what life would be like for Shania who would be required to act as a mother to two little ones before she was out of childhood herself.

Milk and cookies had their timely effect. Tears stopped and Tyrone was soon distracted by a box of colourful building blocks. The three adults looked at each other in turn.

This was real. These children were now their responsibility. There was no turning back.

CHAPTER 16

S hania Devereux woke from a nightmare in which she was being chased down a dark alley by an unknown person, dressed all in black.

She sat up abruptly, and shook her head to dismiss the terrifying images and then found out more frightening things surrounded her. She was in some place she barely recognized in the early morning light coming through a window.

Where was she? Where were the children?

She looked around and gradually remembered the pretty lilac room with the desk and dressing table. The mirror hanging above the dressing table showed a thin, pale girl with disordered hair that seemed to overwhelm her face, clutching the bedclothes to her chest and looking as if she had seen a ghost.

With a shock, she recognized herself.

Is this what I look like? They call it looking like a deer in the headlights. I saw mom looking like this once or twice when things were going badly with him. She must have felt scared like I feel right now.

Is she ever coming back? What will happen to us?

Suddenly she noticed how quiet this house was. There was none of the hustle and bustle of the Children's Home. No feet rushing down the hallway. No children crying.

No children crying!

She was on her feet and grabbing for a sweater. Where were her brother and sister? She rushed out of the room and was faced by a corridor with a bewildering number of doors. She listened and heard nothing.

Did all the people go and leave me here alone?

She did not dare to open doors in case she upset someone. The stepdad hated to be disturbed when he was sleeping off something or other.

She would try the kitchen. Her mom was usually to be found there. The woman ....Louise? She might be there. Hopefully, the man who showed her the lilac room would not be there. She was wary of men, especially when she was alone with one. This man was a stranger.

Tiptoeing down the stairs was interesting. She noticed the huge chandelier light hanging down from the high ceiling and the soft carpet underfoot. This place was like a movie set.

What do these rich folk want with a passel of little kids like us?

It was easy to find the kitchen. She smelled the coffee first. The Louise woman was standing looking out at the back yard with a big mug of steaming coffee in her hand.

Shania moved forward on bare feet and was almost right behind the woman before she sensed something and turned.

"Oh, there you are, Shania! Did you sleep well? The children are still asleep. I'm afraid it was a long night and they did not settle for ages. Perhaps they needed you? But I am glad you had a chance to rest.

There have been a lot of changes lately for all of us."

Louise did not give Shania a chance to answer, so instead she watched.

Very posh dressing gowny thing. Quilted and long. No makeup. Pretty hair. Nervous, but talking to me as if I am a grownup. That's OK. Where's the older lady at? She seemed to know what was what.

"I don't suppose you drink coffee. Would you like hot chocolate instead? Or tea perhaps?"

"Chocolate would be nice."

The woman bustled around the kitchen, opening a cupboard and displaying an array of cans and packets of all kinds from which she extracted a tub of Cadbury's. It was Shania's favourite.

She added boiling water to a large mug and topped it off with cream and a handful of small marshmallows.

Hmmm! She has some idea about what kids like. Good.

"We'll have breakfast shortly, Shania. My husband, Dennis, goes off to work soon. He usually has cereal and coffee. He's not a big eater in the mornings. Would you like cereal now or later? Perhaps you want to have a shower first? You can take your drink with you if you like."

Again with the talking, and no chance to answer or ask any questions of my own. She'll learn soon enough. That's if we are here for a while.

She took the option of leaving the kitchen, mug in hand and climbed the stairs again. She found a lovely washroom near her room and went in, locking the door behind her and running the water in the shower before anyone else could say 'me first!' and claim it.

She let the steaming heat run over her from head to toe and hoped it would wash away the nightmare and the uncertainty and the fear. If they could all stay here for a little time, it would be very nice. It was a big house in a quiet place. She would ask her questions and get answers but for now, it was good to rest in safety.

Mavis arrived at the Ridleys as soon as she saw Dennis's car depart for the day. He must be working shorter hours which was a good idea.

She found Louise in the kitchen, dressed and combed and immediately asked how the first night had gone.

"It was pretty bad, Mavis. You were right about regression. The little ones behaved like babies, thumbs in mouths and all. Dennis helped me rock them to sleep and we finally put them together in the ante room where we could watch them sleep. They were exhausted, poor lambs!"

"What about you? Did you get any rest?"

"Yes, I did, after a lot of thinking. If you can see me through the morning routine, Mavis, I will feel more prepared for the day."

"Of course, I will. What about Shania?"

"I spoke to her earlier. She's not saying much, but

no outright issues. She's in her room. I guess she needed time to herself. I imagine she has been with the young ones all the time since they left their home."

"Of course! Good decision to let her have a bit of space but she will be your best source of advice as to what Tyrone and Betsy like. You will all need routines established as quickly as possible. Let's see how the little ones are doing."

They met Shania on the upper hallway. She was very quietly opening doors and obviously looking for her brother and sister.

"Don't you look nice, Shania. That colour of blue really suits you. I am glad you found the new clothes. The children are in here. Come with us."

Tyrone was curled up on the floor around his teddy bear and just waking up. Betsy was in the bed tangled up in bedclothes, showing she was a light sleeper. She opened her eyes and saw strangers and was about to bellow when Shania surged forward and took her up in her arms.

"Hello, my little girlie! Come with Shanny, now. Everything is all right. The nice ladies are here with us. We'll get you dressed and then we can eat and play."

Louise went to Tyrone, and Mavis showed Shania the change table in the corner. It had been her advice to Louise to dress both youngsters in diaper pants in case of accidents. Shania knew what to do and talked away to her sister while she was washed and dressed. Louise watched and waited for her turn with Tyrone.

Mavis stood back and watched the scene. It was important that Louise cope with everything as soon as possible. She was ready with any advice that might be required, but it was going to be Louise's show and she had to run it.

When the children were fed, and settled in the playroom, Mavis took Shania aside.

"Well done, Shania! I can see you will be an invaluable help to Mrs. Ridley. Do you know that I live next door? There's someone there I would like you to meet. It's all right. Mrs. Ridley knows. We won't be too long. We'll take the private entrance through the treeline.

Shania followed along without expecting too much. The first thing she noticed was the size of the house with the towers at the side. It was even bigger than the Ridley place. They walked along a side path to the front door and were almost bowled over by two big dogs exiting with their owner at the same time.

"Oh, you must be Shania! These two are Oscar and Astrid. It's all right to pet them if you want. You could come for a walk with us soon, if you like. Bye for now!"

In a flash of furry tails the trio were off.

"Is that who you wanted me to meet? What kind of dogs are those?"

Shania's eyes were wide with surprise. Mavis laughed.

"Those are Vilma's dogs. She'll tell you all about them. They walk in the woods behind the house every day. The person I want you to meet is in here.

Mavis knocked on the door on the left of the main entrance and a young voice said, "Come in!"

Shania went ahead with Mavis's encouragement and found herself in the last place she expected. It was a teenager's room with posters on the walls and a pale carpet covered by bright rugs. There was a piano against one wall and, of all things, a cat sat on top of it. There was a big soft couch with throws over it and on the couch sat a girl with a laptop and earplugs, the new kind that had electronic connections.

She put the computer down, unplugged, and stood up with her hand outstretched.

"Pleased to meet you, Shania! I'm Faith Jeffries. Welcome to the neighbourhood. I will be your local guide. I hope we will be friends. I came here from the foster system. I've made all the mistakes you can imagine, so you can ask me anything. I'll tell you the real truth. I promise you that!

What music do you like? You can borrow mine if you want.

Don't say anything to anyone, but I have a private supply of snacks here. Help yourself!"

Mavis heard the last of this as she withdrew and went to find Hilary. Shania was in good hands.

Faith would help her integrate into Westmount Elementary School which shared a large open space with Saunders Secondary. There was no one better to keep an eye on the new girl. All the schoolchildren knew about Faith. She was quite the celebrity these days. As soon as the word was out that Shania was under her protection, everything would go smoothly.

Mavis breathed a sigh of relief.

One down. Two to go.

CHAPTER 17

By the end of the first week, Faith had made a real impression on Shania. She considered her to be *very cool.* Faith advised her on clothes, recommended a good haircut and told her all about Westmount, the mall, and the general types of kids who went to the schools there. There was even a Beauty School in the mall, which caused Shania's heart to beat faster. Faith could not have known it, but she always aimed to work in a salon one day.

Faith promised to take Shania to the mall on the weekend and introduce her to her group of pals.

"Most of them have younger kids in the family who go to Westmount Elementary. We'll set you up with them when the new term begins."

Shania could hardly wait. Now that Louise was

taking over most of the care of the little kids, she could start to think about herself for a change. Ever since the police took away her mom and stepdad, she had glued herself to Ty and Betsy. She knew she was their anchor but she also knew, as weeks went by, that an anchor is a very heavy weight to bear and can drag a person down.

The Ridleys came just at the right time to save her. Now she could think about herself and school was a new beginning. The question remained about how long she would be able to stay with the Ridleys, and with Faith.

In the early morning, she watched out of the window of the lilac room to see the comings and goings next door at the Tower House. Vilma and the dogs went out first, followed by a tall, serious-looking older woman who drove away shortly after, but not every day.

Mavis, she recognized at once. She headed straight to the back of the property and stayed there for hours at a time when she was not with Louise and the kids.

A couple also left by car shortly after that. They did not look like the average Canadian. They had nice tanned skin, dark hair and could be related to each other as they looked so alike. She noted there was at least one man in Faith's house. She wondered what kind of house it was to have so many different people living inside.

At this point in the morning, Shania gave up her watch and got dressed to go down for breakfast with Ty and Betsy. Louise had told her the kids always seemed a little unsettled until they saw their big sis.

Anchor becomes security blanket, she thought.

It was okay with her. She would always feel responsible for these two no matter what happened.

She was also very grateful to Louise and Dennis for keeping the three of them together. Faith told her this was unusual in foster situations. The idea of being separated from the kids and not knowing where or how they were, was horrifying to her.

Faith had not yet told her the story of her own foster experiences but she did say she had an aunt who saved her in the end and who also lived in the Tower House.

So many new people and new stuff to learn, but it all centres around school. If I can make a go of it there, maybe I can stay here forever. Maybe?

She was wise enough to know these big decisions were no longer in the control of anyone over whom she had any influence. It was something to keep in mind.

~

Saturday eventually came around and Faith arrived at the Ridley house to collect Shania.

"Have fun!" said Louise, while quietly placing folded money in the pocket of the new spring jacket Shania wore.

Faith assured Louise she would look after Shania, then the two were off and walking to the nearest bus stop.

"We'll go by bus. You need to know how to get around and how to get to town and back. We'll just do school and the mall today."

Shania felt super cool going out with Faith. She explained that the crescent was a real nice place but not typical of everywhere in London. Shania refrained from saying she understood that. The building where she and the kids had lived before, was a dump compared to anything she had seen on the crescent. Some people would have called it a slum.

As the bus wound its way to Oxford Street and Byron, Faith pointed out the places of interest. It seemed like a long way to the school and Faith said she was hoping to get her driving license one day and then the drive would be much shorter.

Does she mean she would give me a ride to school? Does she think I will be here that long?

The bus turned a corner at traffic lights and

Shania saw the big, brown bulk of Saunders on the left, opposite a long mall with buses arriving and departing in front of it. Their bus deposited them right at an entrance to Westmount Mall and Faith made Shania turn around and see Westmount Elementary, set further back from the road, but very close to the Secondary School building.

She felt glad she was not yet required to take on that challenge. *Soon enough!*

Faith did a walk around the two floors of the mall with comments about what was new and what had recently closed down.

"There's still a Tim Hortons in the centre and in the parking lot at the back is a huge Cineplex movie theatre complex. But what I want to show you today is the Beauty School. The students there will give you a good haircut for a cheap price. They work under their teachers' supervision. What do you think? Is it time for a new look?"

Shania was willing to take her new friend's advice. She reached into her pocket and withdrew the money Louise had thrust in there.

"No! No! This is Mavis's treat."

"Really! Will you come with me?"

"Sure I will!"

There was a large sign on the glass window stating, 'Walk-Ins Welcome'. Before she could change her mind, Shania took one deep breath and took them at their word.

It was like a normal hair salon only there were more work stations than usual and there were a lot of young girls and men working on different customers who were all older. Faith talked to the woman behind the desk and Shania was soon shown to a seat in front of a big mirror. She was glad this seat was not near the front windows so people could not look in while she was sitting there being worked on.

Over her head, a conversation commenced about what might suit Shania. She took no part in this conversation, allowing Faith to take the lead. Although she had seen salons before she had never actually entered one.

Faith stepped back and the young assistant lifted Shania's long curly mop and moved it here and there while examining the effect in the mirror. Next, she moved Shania to another station and wet her hair in a basin after which she encased the dripping mound in a towel and wheeled back to the original spot.

When her hair was towelled dry, Shania saw the scissors in the assistant's hands.

She looked around nervously for Faith and saw her nod with approval.

If Faith was in charge, Shania could relax.

She actually closed her eyes for a while. She could hear the sound of clipping and she knew the assistant was moving back and forward from one side of the chair to the other but she did not see what was happening until Faith tapped her on the shoulder and asked what she thought.

"Should we go a bit shorter?"

Shorter? I have no hair left! What just happened? What have I done?

Shania turned her head to left and right and still could not recognize herself. Her long, curly-brown locks had gone, and what was left was straighter with a slight wave and cut close to her head. A wispy fringe of hair brushed her forehead and longer wings of hair clung to the sides of her face.

Was this a real hairstyle or something partly done?

She looked once again at Faith for reassurance and saw the beaming smile on the older girl's face.

"I think we'll leave it as it is. The cut is good and it makes her look more mature. You can see the shape of her head and the way the hair curves around her cheeks draws attention to those cute hazel eyes.

Shania, you will make a great first impression with this sharp hairstyle. Let's go for a latte and see what the reaction is."

The bill was paid and a tip given to the assistant.

Shania managed a thank you but she was reeling from the shock the haircut made to her self-image. She could feel tiny bits of hair clinging to the skin around her neck and wanted to reach up every minute to feel if she really had lost all that huge clump of hair that she had owned for so long.

They sat at a table in the centre court of the mall and Shania tried not to think everyone else was looking over at her and wondering why she had subjected herself to such a radical change. She sipped her latte and attempted to concentrate on what Faith was saying.

"…….. so, Jolene is my best friend. She has a younger brother at Westmount Elementary. He is an OK kid and they live nearby. Jo will meet us here. I can't wait to see her reaction to your haircut! You know, Shania, it really does make a huge difference. People will treat you like a smart kid now you look like one. I think you have been hiding behind that hair for a long time. I did the very same thing. Mine was dyed green at the ends, if you can believe it?"

Shania nodded as if she believed Faith's story, but what was described did not match with this confident older girl she now saw before her. She began to worry if her own brother and sister would recognize her after such a radical change to their big sister's appearance.

If they ran screaming away from her, it would not be good. There were already too many changes for the little ones to get used to.

Faith started to wave at someone approaching from the main entrance and Shania saw this cute girl with really black hair and blue eyes coming toward their table.

This must be her. Jo something?

There was a big hug, as if Faith and Jo had not seen each other for ages. The talk started up at once and it was like Greek to Shania who did not know the people they were discussing.

"Anyhoo! enough about all that! I want you to meet Shania. She's staying next door to Harmony House, like I told you."

"Hey there! Pleased to meet you. J.J. told me a lot about you. Any friend of hers is a friend of mine. Did you know this one is famous around these parts? She speaks at other schools and does a lot of good work for mental health with teens."

"Hush up about all that, Jo! Shania doesn't need to hear about it. Tell her what you think about her new haircut."

"Right you are!"

To Shania's embarrassment, Jo stood up and walked around the table examining Shania's head from all angles, causing her eyes to go wide and her eyebrows to shoot up as she looked at Faith hoping she would tell the other girl to sit down at once. She knew her face was turning red. She was not used to this type of close inspection.

"Well, I have to say she's a beauty all right! The cut is sensational and it will only improve when it gets a little longer. Wait till the other girls in grade six see it! They will all be clamouring to get into that salon and get the Shania Cut. Well done you two!"

Faith grinned from ear to ear and Jo went off to the counter to get her drink.

"Does she mean it?" Shania whispered.

"You bet she does! One thing you need to know about Jolene is that she tells it like it is. She sorted me out right away when I arrived at Saunders and she continues to keep me in line ever since."

Shania was relieved that Jolene did not ask her questions about her foster situation. She guessed Faith (what was the J.J. about?) had filled her in previously. It was nice to just sit at the table with two older girls and be accepted, even though she could not take part in their chatter about teachers and friends and homework assignments.

By the time the pair's attention finally came around to her again, Shania had lost some of her shyness, and was prepared to provide answers when

Jolene asked what her favourite subject in school was.

"Recess is my favourite, but I suppose I am best at gym since it doesn't matter if you have missed a lesson or two."

Faith immediately recognized a pattern she was familiar with. During episodes when her mother was sick, or drugged, or out of her head, she stayed home also. She saw Jo's quirked eyebrow at this response and countered with, "Well, you will get lots of physical activity now. Your little guys need to be outside playing every day and you have the choice of helping Mavis in her garden or Vilma walk her dogs *and* I have a job for you."

"A job? I am too young!"

"I used to watch a neighbour's younger boy while she was busy with his older brother. I don't have the time to do it anymore, but you could take over for me. It's not a total babysitting job as you would not be alone with the children. It's like a 'mother's helper' and I know Mrs. Wyatt would appreciate your help in the evenings, especially on the weekends. You have way more experience with kiddies right now than I ever had when I started, and it gives you a bit of pocket money. The Wyatts are two houses over in the crescent. I'll introduce you to them."

Shania blinked rapidly. This was all happening so fast. One minute she was standing in their old kitchen, shaking from head to toe as police and social services stormed in and took her mother and stepdad away in handcuffs while Ty and Betsy screamed at the top of their voices and Mom cried out to Shania to 'look after my babies!'

The next minute, it seemed, she was in a new place with new people and suddenly new friends who cared about her. It was almost too much and for a moment she was overcome with the shock of the huge adjustment all this required. Her throat went dry and her eyes stung. She reached up to pull her hair around her face as she used to do to hide herself, but that option was gone now. Her hair and her whole life was changed out of all recognition and she was adrift.

Faith caught the startled expression on her face and reached out a hand to steady her.

"It's okay, Shania! It will be fine. Give it all time. Me and Jo and others will help you. Finish your drink and we'll go across the road and walk around the school so you can see the playgrounds behind it.

One step at a time, really works!"

CHAPTER 18

Mandy Lennox could hardly believe how fast she and her cousin were settling into life at Harmony House. The weather was wonderful, the people in the house were amazing and their shared room was working out fine. It was large enough that the twin beds could be placed against two opposite walls for privacy and still left enough room for a large desk.

Not that the amount of desk space was ever going to be a problem. Since Honor had invited them to share her lower level work and living area, they relished the chance to take breaks outside in the garden or sit on the patio and enjoy the flowers and plants that sprang to life like magic under Mavis's care. When they discovered the elevator just outside the kitchen, it was perfect for dashing down to see Honor without disturbing anyone. Mandy noticed Braden was the one who preferred working with Honor and she was beginning to sense that it was not just about the outdoor access. He and Honor had business experience in common as well as a type of personality match that drew Honor out of her natural reticence.

Whenever Mandy went to the hospital to spend time with her mother, she knew Braden was not only taking care of their business interests, he was also taking care of, what appeared to be, a personal interest.

~

"So, what is this Honor like?"

It was a way to distract her mother from the chemo injections that were of a type that required daily monitoring and various blood tests. Mandy had plenty to relate with all that went on in Harmony House.

"Well, she's very nice. She's knowledgeable about business, works hard and wants to be helpful to us.

Braden sure likes her but the funny thing is that she has a niece who lives in the house too. All the women are of different ages but it seems strange to include a teenager as well. There will be a good story behind that choice, I do not doubt.

Mandy adjusted the cool-pack on her mother's head. It was a new idea to prevent hair loss. Maureen had jumped at the chance to try it as she had a head of gorgeous, shiny, dark hair, much like her daughter's hair, that was truly her crowning glory. The experimental program for this type of breast cancer required Maureen Lennox to remain in the hospital, during in its early stages. Later, if all went well, Mandy and Braden would be able to take her for outings and for overnight rests. For now, she was subjected to blood tests and scans on a daily basis which restricted her movements and tired her body. The lively events at Harmony House occupied her mind and gave her something to think about other than the worries the treatment caused.

"Remember I told you about the woman with the dogs? Right, the same one who invited me and Braden to Jamaica and arranged this whole exchange thing? Well, it seems her romance with the hunky younger guy in the beach villa has fallen apart. I don't know all the details, yet, but there was something about a house that disappeared and caused disappoint for her. The strange thing is, he comes by once in a while and cuts the lawn and takes the dogs out to his place in the country. Mavis tells me this Andy is a great guy who runs an animal shelter and training program but she won't say more than that. There's a lot of loyalty in Harmony and that's a good thing. I can't wait until you can get out of here and meet them, Mama."

"Whenever that happens, I will be well prepared with all your stories. It's better than a soap opera on television, believe me!"

As Mandy emerged from the hospital parking lot she was faced with multiple lanes of fast traffic on Commissioners Road. She went with the flow and connected with Oxford Street eventually. As time went by, she tried other exits and soon became familiar with White Oaks Mall and, by heading in the opposite direction, with downtown London.

She was invited to have lunch with Hilary's son, Desmond, one day in May, and looked forward to the outing.

They ate at The River Room, a charming restaurant within Museum London with a delightful view over the conjunction of the three forks of the Thames River.

Desmond Dempster was a man on a mission, as Mandy soon discovered. He wanted to know what the cousins had been working on in Manitoba with a view to incorporating anything useful into his present employment situation.

"I was at the heart of many business ventures in Toronto for most of my career but I lost touch with the movers and shakers when I made the move to London to be closer to my widowed mother."

"That would be Hilary? I can't imagine her needing much support. She strikes me as a very capable and energetic lady."

Desmond quickly backtracked. This exotic-looking young woman was, apparently, more observant than her youth would indicate. She would not be easily fooled.

"Of course, you are right about my mother, but there was a period during which I had some concerns about her decisions around the co-housing matter as it required a considerable investment of my father's money."

Okay, now I have the true picture! Greed was your motivation.

"Again, Desmond, I think you have no need to be worried. Harmony House is well named. My cousin and I have experience of several types of co-housing establishments and I can assure you this one is a credit to the whole idea of mutual support and friendship."

"Oh, of course! Of course! But, you must admit,

some of the residents are not your typical co-housing types. There's a young girl in a room I know was set aside for a guest suite, and others who I would say are too young to mix with my mother's older age group."

"I hope you are not including my cousin and myself in that category, Desmond? We are a similar age and working type as Honor Pace who runs her business successfully from Harmony House and contributes financially, both for herself and for her niece."

Desmond now knew he had gone too far in his attempt to justify himself. He delivered his final blow to attempt to divert his lunch companion back to business matters.

"I believe you and Braden are, of course, temporary residents, occupying a room recently vacated because of the death of one of the original six women in the house."

This comment served to turn Mandy Lennox totally against one Desmond Dempster. He was trying to shock her into compliance by revealing a secret. Little did he know, Hilary had informed the cousins about Eve's story shortly after their arrival.

Now she felt both annoyed and played for a fool. The lunch ploy was not worth spending more time with this nasty man. She quickly made her excuses and left the museum to walk rapidly along the footpath by the Thames River where she could calm herself down in the more amenable company of ducks and geese before hailing a cab to take her to the hospital. She was determined never again to accept an invitation of any kind from Hilary's son and she would tell the same to Braden.

How on earth did a fine, upstanding woman like Hilary Dempster produce a man like Desmond?

Braden Santiago left most of the hospital visiting to his cousin, at her request. He planned to be more active once his Aunt Maureen, known as Mo in the family, had survived the initial intense period of treatments. Mandy was so good with her mother. The two of them were thick as thieves and always had been. He knew his aunt was in the best hands to speed her recovery.

In the meantime, he was happy to have the chance to confer closely with Honor Pace who had spent her work life in isolation and who was, as a direct consequence, further advanced in internet communication skills than either he or Mandy. Honor had regularly-scheduled, face-to-face business conferences with experts in investing. She attended online seminars given by entrepreneurs from all over the world. All this was accomplished from her office desk where there were several screens supplying multiple types of information simultaneously.

As soon as Braden grasped the scope of this operation, he realized Honor's dedication to working alone was one of her chief advantages. She had few interruptions and a supremely quiet environment around her. She overlooked a serene garden and restful patio. If she chose to connect with someone in the middle of the night, on the other side of the world, she could pop out from her bedroom and commence working without one other person being disturbed.

Compared to what he had known with Mandy by his side, in a lively building housing many others with diverse interests, this was business heaven. Not only was the space perfect, but Honor was also provided with most of her meals from the superb kitchen on the second level of the house. She helped out with clean-up duties in return for healthy food. If she was working through mealtimes there was always a plate left for her in the capacious refrigerator. She also had the usual coffee station and snacks, available in her mini fridge, and was happy to share those with Braden.

AFFINITY HOUSE

To his further surprise, he discovered Honor was a yoga fan. This accounted for her healthy complexion and trim figure. She was not tall but she packed a lot into that neat body and mind.

In fact, as the weeks passed, he grew increasingly aware that Honor was more than happy to share her expertise and time with him. He wondered if she was, basically, a lonely person?

During a break, she proudly told him part of the extraordinary story about her niece, Faith Jeffries, who was the young girl he had seen around the house occasionally. He responded that it was a story worthy of a book to be a useful supplement to the good work Faith was doing with teenagers.

She did not disagree with him about this idea, but insisted she was not going to be the one to write that book.

In spite of this family connection, there was no one else who entered Honor's conversation with him. She was always welcoming when he appeared, mostly when Mandy was with her mother.

They had a quick stroll around the garden, on his insistence, and Honor pointed out the changes effected by Mavis Montgomery.

Once they sat together in a bower at the top of the garden, facing the house, where rose buds were waiting for June's heat to burst into full bloom. It

225

was here he told her how he and Mandy had travelled from South America to find a new life in Canada. She said it was a brave act to set out into the unknown, but privately he thought her own life was far braver and more risky. Perhaps all those who left the familiar behind them and ventured afar were duplicating the journeys of our ancestors who moved out of Africa millennia ago to seek new homes. Today's world travellers had it much easier in his opinion.

He began to speculate about the possibility of winkling one Honor Pace out of her office to venture into London for a meal sometime. It would require delicate manoeuvring, of course, but it would be interesting to see her in a different setting.

Mandy's recent lunch fiasco in the downtown restaurant had drawn his attention. It sounded like an ideal spot for a tête-à-tête.

He imagined he could provide much better company than the dreaded Desmond Dempster, any day of the week.

CHAPTER 19

When Braden Santiago scheduled his meal times to coincide with those of Honor Pace, the rumours began to fly.

"Normally, I avoid the laundry facilities during daytime while Honor is working, but I had muddy jeans from the veg patch I was weeding and they needed immediate soaking.

When I went in through the open glass patio doors, they were head to head over one of the screens and I swear their faces were touching."

"Well, now, that is something different for Honor. How did they react when they saw you?"

"That's the strange part, Hilary. They didn't even budge an inch. I walked past and it was not until Honor heard the water running into the washing machine that she turned her head to see me. She just smiled and went back to her conversation with Braden."

"Really? Our shy little Honor? Our workaholic?"

"I hesitate to predict, but it may be we have a romance on our hands."

"Who could blame her? That Braden is absolutely gorgeous! What surprised me is that he hasn't been snatched up already."

"True! Good luck to them I say. Honor could use a happy connection in her life. She works too hard."

Something of the same conclusion had occurred to Braden. One sunny afternoon when they were sitting in the shade on the stone patio sipping frosty coffee drinks, he ventured to ask a personal question.

"So, Honor, what do you do for fun?"

The question stunned her. Her mouth fell open and her brain raced to try to come up with an answer.

What did she do for fun?

This was a new concept. What she did to earn money would have produced a swift response. What she did to support her niece ....no problem with those details.

But fun? *Where did fun fit into her life?*

This was embarrassing. She pretended to choke

on the cold drink and occupied herself with mopping up the spilled coffee that dripped down her chin.

Braden was not deceived. Her lack of an answer gave him all the information he needed.

"I think it's important to balance out the hours we spend in mental activity with something to feed the soul. Something creative. For me, it's music."

"Really! Do you sing?"

"Like a frog, I'm afraid! Mandy has a sweet voice. I play the pan pipes; a kind of flute. They're very popular in South America and easy to carry from place to place. This garden would be a great spot to practise in."

Braden's words revived a memory Honor thought was buried in her distant past. When she was packing her case to run away from home, the last thing she stuffed in among the clothes was a thin, silver, treble flute, in its leather case. She bore no great love for the instrument. She had disliked the lessons shared with her twin, but the flute was the only item of any value that Felicity might sell for drugs. Some vague idea of protecting her sister by removing it made her take it away with her.

Like everything connected to that desperate period of her life, she had done all she could to forget it, to bury it deep. Until Faith's unexpected arrival, she had been successful in that attempt. Dredging up a past of which she was bitterly ashamed had been painful but, with respect to Faith, it was ultimately worthwhile.

Was this latest reminder to be another positive, or just a brief distraction along the way? In either case, she had no intention of sharing her sordid past with Braden Santiago, a man who had breezed into the life of Harmony House and was just as likely to breeze out of it again as soon as his purposes were met.

She looked up and found his dark gaze intent on her face.

He was still waiting for a response.

Flustered, she rushed into a sanitized version of her thoughts.

"You reminded me that I have a treble flute somewhere in the storage area locker. I used to play … but not very well! It's years since I thought of it at all. It's probably beyond recovery by now."

"So, a fellow musician! Wouldn't this lovely garden benefit from the strains of pipes once in a while? It would make a nice break from our more intellectual pursuits. Please do have a root around and see if you can find your flute, Honor."

She gave a noncommittal half-smile in response and fervently hoped to hear nothing more about it.

The last thing she wanted was to be distracted from serious work by an outdoor concert consisting of two flutes and Mandy's flute-like voice. *What a spectacle that would be?*

She shuddered. A lifelong habit of trying to avoid public scrutiny was not about to be discarded on the whim of one man, even one as good-looking as Braden Santiago.

She meant to add no further fuel to his fire. She sprang to her feet and headed back inside the house, leaving him with the impression she was keen to start the search for the flute at once, but she was firmly settled behind her computers and hard at work by the time he followed in her footsteps.

Ah, well! There's still the chance of a nice lunch downtown one of these fine days. I won't give up that easily. Honor Pace does not yet know how persistent I can be. I owe her something in return for all she has generously shared with me in her work area.

⁓

Jannice O'Connor was keeping secrets from the others at Harmony House.

This was not difficult to do. For one reason or another, the house was in such an uproar most of the time these days that one small person's silence was hardly noticeable.

It seemed as if Life was rushing ahead to fill in the gap left by Eve's passing. Her room was given over to two strangers, her bed was gone, and her paintings were dispersed. Even in her kitchen, cupboards had been rearranged and her systems changed. Jannice still expected to find Eve busily mixing ingredients or storing supplies, or pulling something tasty out of the oven with those massive red oven gloves she wore, but the kitchen now lacked her cheery presence and it could never be replaced.

Jannice realized the whole period during which Eve was dying under her care, was traumatic for her.

Of course, it was not the first time she had watched over a dying client's last days and comforted the family members, but, this one was too close to home. She knew Eve in a way she did not know her assigned clients. Every stage of deterioration she observed in Eve was one she could expect, and for which her training prepared her. But Eve was more than just another client. Eve was one of the adopted family members Jannice had acquired when they all entered Harmony House together. Eve was one of the younger members. If Eve could be gone so soon and so completely, it meant anything could happen at any time. It meant life was truly uncertain and unpredictable.

This realization was slow to grow but when it did, it threw Jannice into a tailspin. Her general distraction was noticed at work and she was asked if she needed some compassionate leave.

"This kind of work often takes a toll on carers, Jannice. Take some time off. I know you have been helping a friend to do some research in the Toronto area recently, but perhaps it's time for you to concentrate on yourself for a change. Travel or sit quietly. You will soon know what you need. We'll be here when you are ready to return."

Her supervisor was a compassionate woman who knew what was needed before Jannice did. She took off her uniform and hung it away in the back of her closet. Then she stopped.

What next?

She needed something, or someone, to fill the gap.

Her thoughts went to Vilma but Vilma was not readily available these days. She was immersed in some drama of her own related to Andy, and Jannice knew she did not have the strength to take on Vilma's troubles as well as her own.

She thought of Mavis, who was the most comforting and calming person she had ever known, but Mavis was busy rescuing the three poor children next door at the Ridleys, when she was not in the garden.

For lack of an alternative, Jannice roamed out of doors and into the garden. At first, the flowers Eve had loved and painted so often, brought back the loss in even sharper focus, but as she walked slowly from pathway to raised beds and on into the shade of the forest edge, she felt a calmness descend on her. It was external and physical only, but she was glad to have that, at least.

She brushed the hair back from her forehead and searched for a downed log where she could rest unseen. She found one, leaning against the trunk of a stately fir and plopped down on it, drawing her knees up and clasping them to her. The intervening brush and thin new growth served as a curtain to partially-obscure the rear of the house. From this perspective, the house was less imposing and she was able to view it more impassively as just a building rather than the place holding so many painful memories.

She was reminded of the small house in Old East London where she had lived for most of her life. With Vilma's help, she was able to leave that massive part of her life behind and it had not haunted her since then. Indeed, it impelled her forward to something better at Harmony House to fill the gap.

Was she now ready for another change?

And there it was!

The question that had been wearing away at her nerves and for which she had been using a great deal of her energy to keep submerged beneath the surface.

She could block it no longer.

She was in the midst of change already. Had she really believed everything in her life was settled forever? She had achieved a worthwhile profession and had a small car to provide some independence. This might not seem like much to others with higher ambitions, but to Jannice O'Connor, it was a huge achievement. Why did it no longer seem enough for her? What was the source of this restlessness?

Time for some honesty.

She settled her back more comfortably against the trunk of the tree, pulled down her summer-length shorts to cover her knees, and gave her mind up to her surroundings. Insects buzzed around her on their way to the wild flowers scattered in the grass. Tiny ants went up and down the trunk on their assigned tasks as if on a major highway. The sun dappled the forest floor and released scents of green growth.

She took in a deep breath and pushed it out together with every doubt and fear in her body.

What was holding her back?

She and Mitchell had a wonderful time in Toronto. He was knowledgeable and stimulating company and she was quickly caught up in his search for the authentic locations of the Grace Marks story. There were hours of research in the Toronto Library System and hours watching the recent television series in the hotel of an evening with its unanswered questions adding to the host of unknowns. No one had the complete story of a simple serving girl accused of murdering her employers. Not even Grace Marks herself was sure of what happened.

What Mitchell required of Jannice, apart from a valuable sounding board, were her insights into the mindset of immigrants from Ireland who arrived on these shores with generations of behaviours and traditions related to their feelings about their hated English overlords.

Was it possible, he speculated, that Grace was overcome with deep feelings of resentment deriving from her ancestors? Had she reacted without thought to one unfortunate set of circumstances and condemned herself to fifteen years of imprisonment?

Was she guilty or innocent in the deepest of senses?

Jannice's identification with Grace Marks grew more intense as the hours of investigation grew. Through the stories of her own parents, she knew how Grace must have felt. She endured lowly servitude for her superiors with little respect or consideration for her needs. There would be endless hours of backbreaking work with no thanks, only more and more effort required; a future in which this would never change until she died.

Mitchell was at pains to point out how much better circumstances were today for labourers and domestics but something of Grace Marks had entered Jannice's soul and darkened her perspective.

Was this the change which seemed to threaten her?

Mitchell Delaney was currently concluding his research in Toronto and consulting publishers. A title for his book had been decided: *Irish Influences in Ontario.* He was due to arrive in London for a visit to nearby Lucan to catch up on the Donnellys' saga that took place there in well-documented and tragic circumstances.

Jannice had also arranged for him to meet the young couple who bought her old home. Kathleen and Patrick's family stories could add to his understanding of the period during which Irish settlers came to this part of Ontario and brought with them all the evil deeds of the past to haunt their new lives and ruin their futures.

So then, what would happen when Mitchell departed back to Quebec to work on his book?

Was their association over, once he had squeezed every last piece of knowledge from her?

What was she to him?

What did she wish to be?

He was a charming man with impeccable manners. He had never given her a moment of concern as to his intentions. In truth, she had put up a high barrier between them; a barrier which would have discouraged all but a practised mountain climber.

What would happen if she let down this barrier and allowed Mitchell, the man, to know her more intimately?

Is this what she feared?

Was she afraid of losing him completely when his work was done?

Once that door opened up a crack, many questions flooded through. What sort of relationship was possible? Where would she live? Would he be content with a part-time arrangement allowing her to continue to live at Harmony House? Would Mavis and Hilary be shocked if that were to be her choice?

Jannice O'Connor realized she had made a giant leap of faith in contemplating these questions at all. She also understood that serious changes would inevitably follow.

CHAPTER 20

Vilma Smith was roaming the far reaches of the woods with Oscar and Astrid. She was no longer afraid of losing control of the dogs or of finding herself in unfamiliar territory. Every tree and boggy area was well-known to her now and she relished the chance to escape from the house and wander in peace with her thoughts.

Lately, her thoughts had been troubling. Andy Patterson had moved on. Their brief affair had died a natural death once his attention focussed exclusively on the barn extension and the dog accommodations.

He had not invited her to see the finished premises and she had no wish to do so. Her dream of a cozy home for two had vanished. Living above the old stable block was not her idea of luxury. It suited Andy's casual style very well and gave him instant access to the working barn but it was a step down for Vilma Smith.

He occasionally borrowed her dogs to demonstrate agility or obedience training and she was happy to let him take them in his truck. He was always grateful, but that was as far as it went.

She comforted herself with the knowledge that she had helped restore him to the active, purposeful life he always should have had. Her part in that transformation was over.

She knew he would come running if she ever called on him for help. He owed her that much.

She was gradually becoming content with her simpler life.

No big dramas. No financial worries.

Another winter escape holiday in Jamaica was in her future, and possibly more of the same with an agreeable travelling companion. There were amazing places to visit in the world. There were cruise ships filled with friendly travellers. All the options were available to her now.

She had the dogs for company and the comings and goings of Harmony House for entertainment. There was always something bubbling up there. Brandon and Mandy's arrival had sparked a number of events and she had been responsible for their inclusion in the house, on this temporary basis. She rarely saw the pair but she had heard no complaints. Perhaps this short-term occupancy was the answer for future residents. It certainly added interest.

Just as she was emerging from the deep shade of the woods, she noticed Astrid running off at an angle as if she had spotted a squirrel rummaging for nuts in the undergrowth. She opened her mouth to call the dog back when she recognized Jannice crouched under a tree.

"Hey, there! Everything all right? I almost missed you!"

Jannice awoke from a doze with a wet nose nudging her thigh.

"Oh, it's you, Vilma! I must have fallen asleep for a minute. I was deep in thought."

The confusion that accompanies a sudden awakening impelled Jannice O'Connor to blurt out her feelings in a way she never would at any other time. Vilma was a dear friend. She had bodily moved Jannice O'Connor from a past century into the modern age and she was the one person in the world who could be utterly trusted.

"Vilma, will you come over here and listen to me? I am in need of your good advice."

As her friend spoke out, Vilma became aware of how she had neglected her ever since Eve's passing. They had not spoken about it together and now she felt guilty. The dogs were ready to settle after their exertions and Vilma plopped down on the grass at Jannice's feet, determined to make up for her recent neglect.

"Ask away, my dear. Advice is cheap."

The whole story of Eve and then of Mitchell Delaney poured out of Jannice like a stream long dammed.

Vilma was shocked and surprised at the same time but she concealed her inner reactions and listened attentively knowing that sooner or later Jannice would reach the crux of the matter and she would know where her help was most needed.

She studied the anguished face in front of her and waited with increasing concern.

When the long and convoluted tale finally ended in a teary sigh, Vilma was still confused.

Was Jannice depressed because of Eve? Was she missing Mitchell Delaney? Was she simply feeling unsettled at the moment, or was this something more deep-seated?

"Jannice, dear girl, I know I have been

preoccupied with my own affairs of late and I need to apologize for that. You sound distressed and I have not been there for you.

You asked for my advice today. Truly, I do not know what to tell you in the circumstances. Is it love advice you need? If so, I am presently a sad case. My own romance, of a sort, has fallen apart and I am dealing with broken dreams."

Vilma's confession prompted Jannice to make a comparison with her own thoughts.

"I do think you can help me with this Mitchell situation. You had a romance with Andy that was partly conducted here in Harmony House. It was not an official relationship like an engagement or a marriage, but no one was bothered about that. Is that the way things go these days?"

"Well, relationships come in different forms depending on what is possible at the time. Andy and I had no suitable home together so we did what we could to be together whenever we could manage it. The women here understood our situation and we tried not to be too obvious when we spent a night in my room.

Jannice, tell me. Is that what you want to do with Mitchell?"

"Oh, he can easily afford a hotel room. That's not the problem. But what if he wants me to go and live with him in Quebec City? I would be cut off by distance and language from all I know."

"Has he asked you to do this?"

"No! No! But I think he would if I gave him an opportunity. He's coming to London soon."

"So, then, why not ask him what he intends for the future? You can always say no. And, you can say yes and see where it leads. A night together in a fine hotel in London would answer a lot of your questions."

"Would you think less of me if I did that, Vilma?"

"For goodness sake, no! It's the twenty-first century, Jannice.

I know you had a sheltered upbringing as a child, but today you can design a relationship to best suit you. If that design means you and Mitchell see each other occasionally in Quebec or in London, no one would question it at all. It's entirely your own business."

"Hilary or Mavis would not object?"

"Did you sign a clause in your contract restricting relationships?"

"No."

"Neither did I Jannice. Think about this and make a plan so you can move forward.

As for right now, we should get indoors. All this

245

talking has made me thirsty for a tall, cool, glass of lemonade."

Vilma reached down and pulled Jannice back up onto her feet. The dogs shook the sleep out of their fur and headed for the house and a snack of their favourite crunchy nuggets. Their mistress had left the bowls of water and snacks out before they went on their walk so they knew what to expect.

Funny thing about people. They seemed to need to sit still and talk about stuff for hours, when a good run would sort out most of their problems.

~

Braden Santiago went out to stretch his legs after a long computer session with Honor. He had to admire her work ethic. She never seemed to stop once she was tracking down a good investment opportunity.

He had put aside for now the matter of a music break or a lunch in town but he had not given up on either idea.

Dusk was beginning to darken the sky after another lovely day when he saw Andy Patterson emerging through the bank of fir trees between the houses. Andy was pushing an electric lawn mower and he looked as if he was intending to cut the grass.

Braden intercepted him with a call out.

"Hi Andy! Haven't seen you around lately. You're working long days if this is the time you choose to cut grass. Can I help at all?"

Andy was relieved to see Braden. The two men had grown close during the Jamaican week but in his attempts to avoid a confrontation with Vilma he had been turning up at Harmony House at ever-increasingly odd hours. He was hoping to come and go without encountering anyone from the house or answering their difficult questions.

"Hi Mate! Sorry! I meant to keep in touch but things got in the way. I'll be passing this lawn maintenance work onto a new guy soon. I don't have the time now with the dog business catching on the way it has. Look! If you get a couple of beers, I'll fast-run this machine over the grass and we'll have a good chat about stuff. I want to know how your aunt is managing."

Braden accepted the invitation and went indoors to check the contents of the kitchen fridge. He found Mandy there putting together a platter of cold meats, bread rolls and cheeses. When she understood his mission she insisted on joining him and Andy on the porch.

"Look, Braden, I really want to find out what's going on with him and Vilma. I thought they were a sure thing when we first met them in Jamaica, but since we moved in here he's been absent and Vilma doesn't seem to be missing him."

"Well, come along if you must, but don't embarrass the guy, Mandy. I think he's trying to keep under the radar for his own reasons. He did ask about your mother though, so that's a good excuse."

By the time Mandy had set up the wicker table on the porch with a laden tray and pulled three chairs near enough for comfort, darkness had fallen. She found candle lamps in tall glass containers and lit them for their ambient glow, and to keep mosquitoes at bay. The beer was still cold when Andy returned from stowing the mower in the garages and he drank down most of one bottle before he spoke.

"Good to see you Mandy! How is your mother doing with her treatment?"

This was a neutral topic and would serve to ease the conversation into more personal matters. Later on, Braden asked if he could take over the lawn maintenance for the interim period.

"I am around here for most of the day and it would be no trouble for me to do it. You can give me the key to the garage. I'd appreciate the exercise. Too much hunching over computer screens is not good for me."

"That's decent of you, Braden. It would really help me out. I have a young lad on site at the barn when I am absent but I really prefer to be there in case the bigger dogs get antsy in the evenings."

"No problem! So the business is doing well?"

"Yes. It's a lot of work and long days of training sessions but the new facilities are custom-designed for the purpose and that helps me keep all the balls in the air."

Mandy pushed the platter of food toward him. He looked like he could use a good meal. She took the opportunity to insert an enquiry of her own into the discussion.

"What about that dream house project you and Vilma were talking about in Jamaica? How is that coming along?"

Braden kicked his cousin's nearest ankle under the table and shot her a warning glance that Andy missed while he was putting together a giant sandwich from the platter contents.

Mandy stifled a cry of pain and kicked back at Braden without successfully contacting him.

Andy took a huge mouthful of bread and meat and chewed thoughtfully before he answered.

"That house project had to be put on hold. The insurance money wasn't enough to cover it and I was able to fix up temporary living quarters above the kennels."

Even to his own ears, this sounded like a feeble excuse.

In the pregnant silence that followed his statement, Andy realized he needed to be more open with these two.

"Look! The truth is that you will know more about how Vilma feels than I do. You see her around here every day while I have obviously been avoiding her. How does she seem to you two? Is she okay?"

"She seems perfectly content, as far as I know, Andy. She has her daily routines with the dogs but she doesn't socialize much. I am at the hospital every day and Braden fills in on the work front for me. Do you want me to talk to her?"

"God, no!"

The men's voices spoke loudly, in concert, so Mandy knew this was not going to be an option.

"Fine! I hear you, but I think it's a shame to let something good die a death from neglect like this."

She pushed back her chair and stormed off with her dark hair swinging, leaving Braden to take care of the tray.

"Uh, sorry about that! Mandy speaks her mind, as you just heard."

"She's right of course, Braden. I need to sort this out with Vilma before it's too late.

Thanks for the food and the offer of help. It's only for a few weeks until I hand over the business to another guy. Here's the garage key. Once, every few days will keep the grass under control. Mavis will tell me if anything more needs doing.

I have to go now. My truck is parked at the Ridleys."

Andy ran off across the lawn like a man being chased by demons.

Braden sighed. He really must have a talk with Mandy about interfering, but perhaps he had better wait until she had cooled down.

CHAPTER 21

Louise Ridley heard the noise of the truck starting up and her hand went to her throat.

It had taken two hours to get Ty to sleep and that was accomplished only with Dennis's help. He took Betsy upstairs to play in her sister's room until she collapsed with sheer exhaustion. It always upset Betsy to hear Ty crying.

Shania tucked her sister into her own bed and sent Dennis back to see how Ty was doing. She was now at school every weekday and it was going well thanks to the help from Jo's brother and his pals who steered her straight whenever she ran too close to the established school groups.

It was a great relief to be out of the house for so many hours and able to concentrate on her own life for a change. Not that there was anything wrong at the Ridleys' place.

Mavis spent time there every day, especially while Dennis had to be at work. The two little kids played in Mavis's garden and had occasional visits with Vilma's two dogs. There was a new swing set installed at the Ridley's and Dennis had created a maze structure from large foam panels which he rearranged every day to provide new challenges and reveal unexpected treats or surprises. Ty loved this, but Betsy enjoyed most just sitting in the safe chair swing and rocking back and forth.

Louise gave Shania a full report of their activities every day after school and Shania was pleased to hear how well they were doing. She no longer felt like their mother. That task she relinquished into the capable hands of the adults around her. For now, she was simply relishing being a kid; a kid who had a best friend in Faith Jeffries. Faith was someone who really understood what Shania had been subjected to for months and months while her mother and stepdad lurched from one disaster to another and finally, through their neglect, caused the death of the tiny baby they had created and who was never to make it to his first birthday.

When Ty screamed with nightmares or Betsy refused to be soothed, Shania knew exactly what they were remembering. At least, now, she had the compensation of having a part of her life totally removed from all of that horror. School, for all its challenges, was a place that required all her attention. During those hours she was safe from the bad memories. Over time, the effect of school was making the bad stuff fade, just a little. For this she was grateful. Faith said it would get easier. Shania hoped she was as right about this as she was about everything else.

Of course, in the back of her mind lurked the fear that the Ridley situation was only temporary and the whole settling-in business might have to start all over again. Even worse was the prospect of being separated from the little ones; never to know how they were coping or who was looking after them and trying to understanding their specific needs. No one could do this like she could. She coached Louise about how to soothe Ty's skin rash when he was stressed, and about Betsy's hatred of any foods that were red in colour. Louise assured her she was invaluable in helping the children adjust to their new circumstances.

For these reasons, Shania tried to be as helpful as possible to Louise and Dennis. She ate whatever was put in front of her without complaint and took delight in keeping her lilac room spotless. She never asked for school supplies or rides, or clothes. Faith supplied all she needed before she could even ask.

Faith was her confidante. Faith was her security. Faith was the big sister she had never had. Faith was the mother she should have had. Knowing Faith was there in the background allowed Shania to become a teenager who looked like she fit in. She knew she never would actually fit in, but as long as the other kids around her believed she did, she could fake it.

The day Faith told her about the scholarships, was Shania's darkest day since her baby brother died.

She was with Jo and two other boys from the J.J. group. They were having milkshakes after school at Tim's in the mall when Faith dropped the bomb.

No one noticed that Shania felt like fainting at the news. Jo was dancing up and down in delight, the guys wanted to see the actual offers on her phone and Faith was answering five questions at once.

Shania's brain shut down completely. This was her worst nightmare. If Faith left London for one of these colleges out of town, she would be bereft of all help.

Faith finally noticed how pale Shania had

become. She reached across the table and stopped Shania from falling off her seat in a dead faint.

Josh ran to the mall offices to get help. Jo held Shania upright and talked to her while Faith phoned the school and explained the situation. The reply she received was not satisfactory. As Shania was no longer on school property she was not their responsibility. Fortunately, the mall security people quickly responded and Shania was taken to the offices where first aid was administered.

Shania was embarrassed to have caused a fuss but Faith quickly figured out the reason and assured the mall staff that she was capable of taking Shania home to get adult help if they would go outside and find a cab for them in the taxi rank.

She bid a fast farewell to Jo and said she would talk later then the two girls got into the cab and headed for Harmony House. Faith encouraged Shania to close her eyes and rest while she called ahead to alert Mavis.

A tray of strong tea and sweet snacks awaited the pair's arrival. Faith gave Mavis a quick summary of events before leaving them to talk over matters together.

"So what got you so upset, Shania?"

Shania blushed and sipped more of the strong, sweet tea.

"It was nothing really. I feel fine now. I'm not sick or anything. I'll go home now."

"I am sure you are fine but I think you had a shock at the mall when Faith told you about her future plans. Before you deny it, Shania, please know that Faith will not desert you. I will be here and Louise and Dennis are on your side. We are all so proud of the way you are facing the difficulties caused by so much change in your life. You are stronger than you think, my dear. When school finishes at the end of June you will have friends to see you through grades seven and eight and a whole summer ahead in which to relax."

"Thank you, Mavis. I know you are right. It's just worrying every time I feel settled and something else happens to throw me off. It's the uncertainty."

Mavis sucked on her back teeth as she mentally composed her next words. She was aware of recent court events which she had discussed with Louise. They decided to delay informing Shania but Mavis could now see the girl was more mature than they had given her credit for.

"Look, Shania! I realize you are in a difficult position. Louise will tell you more about this, but just know that you will be with the Ridleys for quite some time. The court case about the baby's death has been postponed until more information can be

gathered. It's a matter of deciding who was the more responsible party.

For now, your mother is receiving help and your stepfather is being held in a separate location under supervision. They are forbidden to communicate with you as you will be a witness when the case finally comes to trial. Louise and Dennis are sending regular, very positive reports, about your progress and about how helpful you are with the little ones.

I can see no reason for any immediate changes to this situation, so please do not worry. Faith will be here all most of the summer with you and I believe she has a part-time job arranged for you."

Shania felt a wash of relief that started in her brain and sped through her entire body. She stood upright and the faintness had gone.

"Thank you, Mavis. I'll go on home now. Thank you again for treating me like a grown-up. I really do appreciate being here. I will stop worrying about the future and do my part to help Tyrone and Betsy. Thanks for the tea."

She turned and ran off like the child she still was.

Mavis sighed deeply. This was an interim period in Shania's life but one that could have a huge effect on her future. While the little ones would soon forget their troubled beginnings, Shania was the one who would carry the memories and the effects into

her adult existence. Without very careful handling, Shania could become one of those lost souls seen on big city streets existing on the fringes of society with no support system and no prospects. Education was the key to her survival just as it had been with Faith.

Mavis decided to have a talk with Hilary. It looked like she would be required to take on another pupil this summer. Shania's confidence would grow as her competence in school subjects was improved. This time, Hilary would have the assistance of Faith. Just knowing how Faith had succeeded was the best possible predictor of Shania's success.

Ah, Hilary! When we began this co-housing project we could never have known we would be heading up a school for troubled youth, among other things. I suppose it's good to know we are still useful at our age. Life is full of surprises and, on the whole, that is a good thing all round.

∼

Faith Jeffries left Shania in Mavis's capable hands and headed straight for her aunt Honor. There was a lot to discuss among herself, Honor and Hilary. Which of the three scholarships would best suit Faith's goals and which provided the best financial advantage?

It was enormously exciting to have these choices.

Research was required to compare the options but the final decision must belong to Faith.

Honor would not attempt to persuade her niece in any direction but in her heart of hearts she felt Kingston or a college near that location, would be Faith's choice. Honor took this as a sign that the girl had learned the benefit of having someone within reach who knew her background story and who could keep her on track when the inevitable stresses of higher education brought problems.

Honor knew the Jeffries' filled that bill for Faith. Melvin was already a fan and his mother was a steadying influence on all the children. Mason Jeffries felt an obligation to Faith and he was capable of taking the place of the missing male figure in her life.

A pang of regret swept through her as these thoughts coalesced in her mind but she dismissed that weakness. She had played her part in Faith's resurrection by supplying the missing information about her twin's early life. The bond between them might well be stretched in the coming years but it could never be severed.

Honor walked out to the stone patio and took a moment to let her mind venture into the unknown future. Perhaps, Faith would return here to Harmony House and make her life in London.

Perhaps, she would find a partner in her college years, and marry and raise children in another town. Perhaps, in time, Faith and Honor would find themselves back together again in different roles.

The future was unknowable. The present was full of promise and that was sufficient for now.

~

Vilma noticed Braden pushing the lawn mower around the grass areas and immediately wondered why.

She wasted no time in finding the answer. As soon as he had finished raking the excess grass and bagging the pile for Mavis's compost bin, she was ready with a cool drink and several questions.

"Andy did not tell me to keep any secrets. Mandy and I had a chat with him a few days ago. Mandy was annoyed with his behaviour toward you and she showed it. Andy took off in a hurry after agreeing I could take over this job until he gets someone to replace him on a permanent basis. That's all I know."

Vilma shifted on the wicker seat and pulled a cushion into place to protect her bare back from the sharper sections of the chair. June weather had finally arrived and a sundress with a short skirt was the required attire when out of doors.

"So Braden, what do you think about this situation? You and Andy grew close in Jamaica."

Braden Santiago was conscious of the obligation he owed to Vilma Smith. She had made it possible for him and Mandy to be nearby during this vital phase of Mandy's mother's breast cancer treatment.

Privately, he agreed with Mandy that Andy Patterson had behaved badly but there was the unspoken rule among guys to protect each other, especially when one of them was in the wrong.

Vilma recognized, as the pause grew longer, that Braden was in the midst of a dilemma. He was wiping sweat off his brow with a cotton scarf from around his neck. A typical male delaying tactic.

She was not about to let him off the hook. He could squirm there as long as he liked. She could wait him out.

"Look, Vilma! It's none of my business. You two need to get together and set things right. Obviously, Andy is removing himself from Harmony House but I think he owes you some kind of explanation before he vanishes completely. That's all I'm saying.

Thanks for the drink."

He marched away with the lawnmower in front of him and she knew she would get nothing more from him. He was right and Vilma knew it. This situation was untenable. Andy was taking the coward's way out. She was the mature one and she would write him a letter in preference to turning up at his place of business and risking a rebuke. Whatever Andy decided to do after this, the ball was firmly in his court.

She was the injured party. Her conscience was clear. She was content with her present circumstances so it was up to him to demonstrate what he was made of.

No time like the present.

She rose to her feet and went upstairs, but she had to admit there was a lingering sense of regret that the dream had died in this way. It was her very last attempt to replace her beloved husband, Nolan, in her life. From now on, she would rely on no man.

Dear Andy,

We are drifting further apart with each day that passes.

I know you are now totally involved with your new career and I am happy for you, as you must know.

I believe our relationship has come to an end.

We had some amazing moments together but isolated moments were all we had.

Fate was against us in some ways.

I wish you only the best.

Astrid and Oscar are a daily reminder for me of your love of dogs and your generosity of heart.

Be well. Move on. Know that I bear you no ill will.

Vilma.

She read the letter over once with a tear forming in her eye, but she did not change anything.

She placed the page in an envelope, addressed it and summoned the dogs for a walk to the nearest post box.

Overall, she felt a sense of release. It was done. Andy might not even feel a reply was needed. If that was what he thought, it was acceptable to her.

Either way, it was over.

CHAPTER 22

It was one of those spectacular summers, when rain fell only when needed and clouds formed at nightfall, leaving the skies clear and blue during the long lazy days and well into the fall.

Mavis's garden bloomed like never before. The roses in June were remarkable and when they reappeared in August, they were even more prolific, to her great delight. She supplied bowls of roses to Louise and all the others on the crescent and her admirers begged for a garden tour to see if they could discern how Mavis made the magic.

She allowed them to believe magic was involved but she knew sheer hard work and good fertilizer was nearer the truth. Mother Nature always responded to a willing pair of hands, good secateurs, great garden stock and an eye for delightful juxtapositions of colours.

Mavis was increasingly grateful for the raised flower beds as her knees would not tolerate the constant bending to reach ground level. She could manage to get down all right, but getting up again was neither easy nor painless despite occasional yoga sessions with Honor. She could see the benefits of the exercises but privately she agreed with Hilary that they should have started decades before to get the maximum advantages of flexibility and balance.

Most of the heavy garden work was accomplished in the cool air very early in the morning or just before dark, promoting the illusion that the entire garden was self-sustaining. Hilary knew better and watched over her friend to ensure she did not overextend herself.

"Do you miss Andy's help, Mavis?"

"Not really. The new young man is very willing. It's Andy himself I miss. I guess he is gone forever."

"It looks that way. Vilma never mentions him. She takes the dogs out to parks and nature areas for exercise but as far as I know she goes on her own."

"I suppose it's possible she could meet another dog lover somewhere on one of these jaunts and start up a nice relationship."

"I doubt it. I think the whole Andy episode has

wounded her deeply. She's not likely to risk another disappointment."

"It's altogether too bad! Andy was nice to have around and very pleasant to look at."

"I agree.

So, is Vilma happy? Or should I ask if she is content?"

Hilary hesitated. The women were sitting in the shade on the side porch with gin and tonic in a tall glass jug to share, and the leisure to talk quietly unobserved. Marble, who had taken to following Mavis around since the departure of Faith to college, was curled up asleep on her mistress's knees.

It seemed like a good opportunity for the two who were responsible for the co-housing project to do a look back at the year so far. So much had happened that waiting until year's end seemed impossible.

"It's hard to tell about Vilma. She is the same vibrant and positive person but a little of the shine has gone. Not that she doubts herself. That could never happen. She knows who she is and she seems content or perhaps what I sense is more like resignation."

"I do hope she's content. She has been such a force for good at Harmony House and that continues on. It was her idea to switch things around to allow Maureen to move in with Mandy while she recovers from the cancer treatment. Faith was in Kingston with the Jeffries for several weeks and Brandon loves being in her suite. I suspect he also loves nipping along the porch here to see Honor without anyone knowing about it."

"Mavis! Are you saying there's something going on between those two?"

"Well, what would *you* think? Haven't you heard them practising their music in the garden? I believe when two instruments blend together that well, it says something about the two players."

"Really? I just thought it was a good thing that Brandon got Honor out of the house once in a while and into the fresh air. I never thought further than that."

"Oh, there have been several dates in town. Mandy is responsible for encouraging Honor to buy new clothes. She and Vilma went shopping with her in Masonville with some success."

"I see. Mavis, will this bring disappointment to Honor when the trio eventually goes back west?"

"Who knows? At the very least, the time with Brandon must give Honor the confidence that she can be more than a workaholic. Now that Faith is ready to try her wings, Honor's job is done, in large part.

I hope she will find her own happiness. She deserves it."

Mavis almost knocked over the flimsy wicker table in her eagerness to tell Hilary something related to Honor that had happened recently.

"Oh, I almost forgot about this!"

"Settle down Mavis! We nearly lost the gin and tonic there. What's got you so excited?"

It was one of those things you glimpse out of the corner of your eye and at the time it doesn't mean much but when we were talking about Honor just now, I remembered."

"What did you remember? For goodness sake tell me!"

"Well, last week the service call for the elevator maintenance was scheduled."

"Correct, I made the call. So what?"

"The man who came looked familiar. Later I recalled why. He is the same man Honor recommended to us because he did the maintenance in her old apartment building and they met there and laughed because their last names were so similar. He helped with the wheelchair she needed then."

"Mavis dear, why is this in the least way important?"

"Because, Honor appeared as soon as the man

entered the house. They stood together very closely, I noticed, and they talked and laughed like old friends. She called him Jared and he asked right out if she was still Pace. She said, yes she was and she quite liked her initials so if he wanted to change her last name he was welcome to try as the change would be hardly noticeable.

I moved along the hall at that point but I watched the clock and they were there together for a good half an hour and they were getting along really well."

"That is strange, indeed, Mavis! I can hardly believe our Honor was so forward with this man. Do you think they have been meeting secretly outside the house?"

"I have no idea, but you can imagine they have been chatting together every time the elevator inspection happens. I also think what we said about Braden loosening up Honor was right on the money. She was giving off sparks. Even I could see that. Jared would have to be blind to miss her signals.

I think we have a romance on our hands, Hilary!"

"You may be right about that. Now that you bring it to my attention, I do believe I have heard Honor humming as she moves around the house. It could be a sign of her happiness.

If we do have a romance growing there, it is good to know this Jared is a local man, not from Quebec or Toronto or parts even further away. I would hate to lose Honor Pace completely."

Mavis's story made her friend realize she had become somewhat disconnected from the daily life around Harmony House during the summer and fall. She shifted around in her seat and sipped the refreshing drink. The thought was still a little uncomfortable.

"Mavis, how have I missed all this?"

"You, my dear Hilary, have been occupied with Shania most of the summer. Your tower room windows face the side lawn and you are missing events that take place elsewhere."

I suppose there's some truth in that. I never thought I would retire and take up the tutoring role, not once, but twice!"

"Oh admit it! You have never been so happy. Remember how you started in a classroom helping students one to one in recess or after school. That was when you loved teaching. As an administrator, you were gradually removed from the classroom and now you have had the chance to revisit those happy days of long ago."

Hilary laughed long and hard as she patted Mavis on her shoulder.

"What a cheerful view you have of life, Mavis! Nothing is that simple, of course, but I will say having been through the basics with Faith, Shania's academic problems are not such a shock to me. And, don't forget, I have a good backup person in Faith. Those two girls text and message each other every day and Shania's good attitude to learning depends a great deal on Faith's steady encouragement as well as on her excellent example. When you think about it, Shania and Faith are perfectly placed to help one another and understand each other's situations."

"Of course you are right, Hilary, but back to my original point. Your triumph with Faith has meant everything to Shania. Faith is set on a course for a successful future helping others. Conestoga College will be the making of her. It would not surprise me if Shania followed in her footsteps one day."

"Oh, now, don't compare those two girls! Shania is younger and not at all like Faith in personality. She has a longer road ahead of her and a lot of that will depend on Louise and Dennis Ridley.

Tell me how things are going next door."

Mavis sipped thoughtfully for a moment. It had been a long summer for the Ridleys. Mavis kept a close eye on Louise to ensure she did not become overwhelmed with her new responsibilities. What she observed was how vital Dennis's help was in this enterprise. He had not only taken a parental leave from his work, he had also inaugurated such benefits for other new fathers or adoptive parents in his company.

Rather than losing status at work by doing this, the move impelled him upward in the organization. Great interest resulted in the progress of the fostering experiment at the Ridleys and Dennis now produced an online newsletter with ideas he and Louise had found helpful.

Of course, the couple were lucky to be doing fostering at a time when businesses were searching for ways to make their companies more socially acceptable for employees, and the public in general.

Dennis gladly accepted his company's financial assistance to help Louise with housekeeping so she could spend more time with the two youngsters.

All this passed through Mavis's mind in a flash. Hilary knew about most of it. What she was now asking for was a summary.

"I must say, the Ridleys have been transformed in every way by this experience. The children are Louise's dreams come true and Dennis's participation makes their marriage a joint enterprise for the first time.

The only concern I have is in regard to the future of the children."

Hilary could hear the genuine fear in her friend's voice.

"Do you mean there's a chance the parents might claim them again?"

"I sincerely hope the courts would not be that foolish. I am relaying excellent reports to social services and recommending that the children stay exactly where they are. My sources suggest the mother and stepdad will end up in a custodial sentence for negligence and consistent lying to the authorities. There is the serious criminal charge to be considered; a young child's death caused by their neglect.

I can't promise anything, and it's not my place to do so, but if matters progress the way they have been, there is the chance the Ridleys could be allowed to adopt the little family."

"Was there not a matter of a biological father's claim on one of the little ones?"

"Ah, that *is* a worry. There is nothing impending on that score at the present time. We can only hope the father's circumstances mean he is not a good candidate to claim his child. He showed no interest while they were living in extremely difficult conditions."

In the silence that followed this statement, the women heard the sounds of children playing in the front yard next door. They exchanged glances and smiled at each other. It was a happy sound. Louise's deeper tone of voice rose above the children's chuckles encouraging them to continue with their play.

Hilary and Mavis automatically raised their glasses and saluted each other.

Ten minutes went by in joyful contemplation of the year's successes until Hilary said, "I suppose this year in review must contain the less happy moments in order to be complete."

"Ah, you are thinking about Eve."

"Of course I am. It was wonderful that she ended her days peacefully here in Harmony House but it was a dreadful time for everyone. The first real tragedy we have dealt with."

"I know you are right, but look at how Jannice came through for us then. That was a triumph.

I often feel as if Eve's spirit lingers here. We have her paintings to remind us of how happy she was here, despite everything that went before in her life."

"How is Jannice coping these days?"

"She was quite depressed for a time, which is perfectly natural, but Mitchell Delaney's influence appears to be positive and I am not just talking about his writing prowess."

"Mavis Montgomery! Are you suggesting there's something more than a shared interest in Irish heritage going on there? What next?"

"Jannice confided in Vilma before taking the step to move her relationship with Mitchell to a more intimate level while he was in London."

"But I thought they were just busy catching up with the young O'Connors and researching local history! Are you telling me Jannice was not coming home to sleep?"

"Well, she arrived home quite late some nights but on others she stayed with Mitchell and she does not seem any the worse for it. Haven't you noticed the new energy she has now?"

"Ah, I put that down to her promotion at work. What else have I been missing?"

Mavis searched her memory for items brought to her attention recently.

"Oh, Maureen approached me. She wants to have a meeting with us about her stay here. Naturally, she is very grateful for our flexibility in accommodating her and the cousins, but she is wondering if Eve's old room might be available in the future for return check-ups at the Cancer Clinic. She has reached the end of her treatment and recovery. With a clean bill of health now, she was released to go about her life in Manitoba other than for a scheduled six-month check-up in London."

"I see. Well, that will be hard to predict. I have no problem with her returning when necessary. She is just as delightful to have around as her daughter, and an even better cook. I will miss those spicy South-American dishes when she returns home. The question is whether or not we want to start another search for a co-housing candidate to occupy Eve's old room on a permanent basis?

Remember this also; Faith's suite may well be vacant when she is in residence during term time. We could probably work out something to suit Maureen Lennox."

"That's what I told Maureen. Hilary, how do you feel about the possibility of another woman joining us? Or it could be a man! I must say a man can be useful now and then."

"Seriously, Mavis, I have been thinking about it. Financially speaking, it is a loss if the occupant is not contributing a full share in this enterprise."

"But Eve left us a cushion to cover that eventuality."

"She did indeed. I am not averse to the idea of temporary residents, especially those who are known to us already and who we can be assured will fit in. I feel embarking on a new search would be difficult and time consuming. "

"That's my feeling too, Hilary. You might laugh at this, but it's almost as if the universe has been filling places for us! We would never have selected Faith on our own and without Vilma's input we would never have found Mandy, Braden and Maureen. I have been wondering about the possibility of becoming a stop on the international routes for young entrepreneurs."

"What? How much of that gin have you drunk, Mavis Montgomery? Where did you get such an idea?"

"It's not as outrageous as all that, Hilary Dempster. Look around you. London is a hub for universities, colleges and hospitals. There is a lot of research going on here and the money to support more innovation comes with the constant influx of new blood and new ideas.

You must have read about Superclusters. It's a growing trend in business circles. I'm surprised Desmond hasn't mentioned it."

"Mavis! You are a continual fount of ideas! Are you suggesting Braden and Mandy might go home to Winnipeg and encourage other young people to stay with us for periods of time?"

"It's not impossible, is it? Wouldn't you prefer to live temporarily in a quiet area with amenable people around you rather than in some anonymous hotel room or basic student quarters?"

Hilary laughed out loud and almost choked on her mouthful of drink.

"I suppose you are right! Who could have guessed we might be hosting young people from all over the world instead of quietly meandering our way into old age surrounded by equally old people, as we fully expected when we started this project?"

"Well, haven't we two lived long enough to know very little in life can be predicted with any accuracy, especially nowadays when everything changes at the speed of light? The world is different when you get up every morning, or so it seems."

It could have been the influence of a full jug of gin and tonic that was inspiring the two old friends to think so creatively, or it could have been the euphoric effect of counting their many blessings. Whichever was the cause, it was a memorable conversation that brought a variety of subjects into focus.

"Well, before we get to the giddy stage and need to be helped upstairs, I propose a toast to us for adjusting to so many changes despite our advanced years."

Mavis managed to squeeze enough out of the jug to provide each of them with a final toast but, before they raised their glasses, she touched Hilary on the shoulder and asked for her indulgence for one more minute.

"I feel it is only appropriate for our final toast to include an acknowledgement of this wonderful house that is now our home. When you think about it, and I have done many times, it's almost as if Harmony House has played an active role in our success. This house brings people together who need others in their lives. It keeps them safe within its walls until they can move on to whatever their future requires."

"Mavis, you are talking as if Harmony House was alive! Do you really believe that?"

"Oh, now, if anyone other than you asked that question, Hilary, I would deny it utterly, but you and I have been here from the start and I can't see any other explanation for the way in which the house has expanded to meet the needs of whoever arrives at its doors."

Hilary's eyebrows were raised as she contemplated this unusual point of view. She took a moment to look around her. The tower rooms were to her right. It was true that Faith had been saved from injury in some mysterious way when she climbed up to the top of the tower on a precarious ladder. It was true that the house had wrapped its arms around Eve as she lay dying in her room. It was also true that Vilma had been rescued in the nick of time and returned to the safety of Harmony House in the arms of Andy Patterson when she should have suffered serious damage from a prolonged period in the frozen woods while searching for her dogs.

Was Mavis on to something when she described their house as being much more than four inanimate walls?

Hilary Dempster blinked and resorted to her more familiar frame of mind which relied on practical and perceptible indicators. Mavis's fantastical statements, and the thoughts they had inspired, would require a period of serious deliberation in the cold light of day, without benefit of alcohol, before she would be able to respond adequately.

For now, she simply smiled and left the matter aside. Raising her glass she declared,

"To Harmony House! Whatever it is, we were fortunate to find it when we did and that fortune has been shared with others."

Mavis responded with an addendum.

"To Harmony House, now and in the future!"

EPILOGUE

Andy's letter arrived with the first of the Christmas cards. Harmony House was beginning to gear up for another season of reunions when the winter dining room would be filled to capacity with those who, like Faith, had been absent for some weeks or months.

Mavis piled the cards and letters on the hall table under the large and fragrant rosemary tree.

Vilma collected her pile of correspondence as she returned from walking the dogs around noon.

There was only a thin coating of snow on the ground, but the temperature promised much more from the laden clouds hovering above. Vilma had adopted the habit of a quick noon run to settle the dogs for an afternoon nap so she could help Mavis with whichever Christmas project was currently occupying her mind.

The dogs knew the routine and quickly found their beds. Vilma spread the cards and letters on her desk, sorting out which needed a reply and which were personal cards to display on the shelves of her wall unit.

As soon as her eyes fell on the handwritten letter, she stopped breathing for several seconds.

The blue ink and the large sprawling letters of the Harmony House address were unmistakably written in the style of one Andrew Patterson. Had there been any doubt at all, his identity was confirmed by the business label on the left side of the envelope where a big red barn and the logo; Dogs Trained and Housed in Comfort, commanded attention.

A wave of conflicting emotions washed over Vilma. She sat down on the nearest chair and waited for the chaos to subside. She told herself, in no uncertain terms, that she had settled this matter.

She was content with the way it ended.

She did not require anything further from the man.

She did not want to open up old wounds.

She did not need any kind of Christmas greeting from him for the first time.

Curiosity won out in the end after Astrid, roused from sleep, came over to the chair and wrapped her warm body and long thick tail around Vilma's feet.

She knows how I feel! She will stay in place until I finish this.

It was a further ten minutes until Vilma took up the envelope and slit it open.

Inside was a one-page, handwritten note.

It was too late now to change her mind. She took a deep breath and read to the end.

My Darling Vilma,

You will know by the length of time it has taken me to write this, how difficult it is to do.

I can't begin to apologize. If I did the apologies would never end.

Let me state the few things I can without too much shame.

I owe everything to you. No one else could have been so generous and selfless to me.

You found me when I was almost gone and dragged me back to life.

Because of you, I have hope for the future. There are no words to thank you enough for that gift.

You know where I am.

If you ever, for any reason, need my help, I will come to you without question.

No strings attached.

I think of our brief time together with love.

I will never meet another woman like you.

Thank you, Vilma, from the bottom of my heart.

Always,

Andy.

She folded the letter and placed it in the desk drawer. There was some comfort in his words but she knew she did not need them.

Astrid looked up at her mistress's face and seeing peace there, she unrolled herself and ambled back to her brother's side.

Vilma Smith stretched her arms up to the ceiling, then rose and went about her day in the ever-changing, ever-stimulating environment that was Harmony House.

AFTERWORD

Ruth Hay's fourth series, **Home Sweet Home**, follows the ups and downs of six women attempting to live together for mutual support and safety.

Read Ruth's other series, *Prime Time*, *Seafarers*, and *Seven Days* on Amazon, Barnes & Noble, Kobo, and iBooks.

Also read Borderlines a stand-alone thriller.

www.ruthhay.com

Seven Days Series

Seven Days There

Seven Days Back

Seven Days Beyond

Seven Days Away

Seven Days Horizons

Seven Days Destinations

Borderlines (Standalone)

Borderlines

Home Sweet Home Series

Harmony House

Fantasy House

Remedy House

Affinity House

Visit www.ruthhay.com for links to all of Ruth's stories!

Made in the USA
Lexington, KY
20 July 2018